THE *Patua* PINOCCHIO

by
CARLO COLLODI
Adapted from Carol Della Chiesa's
translation from the Italian

Illustrations
SWARNA CHITRAKAR

MASTRO CHERRY

THE CARPENTER

Found a Piece of Wood
That Wept and Laughed
Like a Child!

He gives it to his friend
Geppetto, who fashions a
Marionette and calls it

PINOCCHIO

CHAPTER ONE

ONCE UPON A TIME, there was a piece of wood. It was not an expensive piece of wood. Far from it. Just a common block of firewood, one of those thick, solid logs that are put on the fire in winter to make cold rooms cosy and warm.

I do not know how this really happened, yet the fact remains that one fine day this piece of wood found itself in the shop of an old carpenter. His real name was Mastro Antonio, but everyone called him Mastro Cherry, for the tip of his nose was so round and red and shiny that it looked like a ripe cherry.

As soon as he saw that piece of wood, Mastro Cherry was filled with joy. Rubbing his hands together happily, he mumbled half to himself: "This has come in the nick of time. I shall use it to make the leg of a table."

He grasped the hatchet quickly to peel off the bark and shape the wood. But as he was about to give it the first blow, he stood still with arm uplifted, for he had heard a wee, little voice say in a beseeching tone: "Please be careful! Do not hit me so hard!"

"Where did that voice come from, when there is no one around? Might it be that this piece of wood has learnt to weep and cry like a child? I can hardly believe it. Here it is—a piece of common firewood, good only to burn in the stove, the same as any other. Yet—might someone be hidden in it? If so, the worse for him. I'll fix him!"

With these words, he grabbed the log with both hands and started to knock it about unmercifully. He set aside the hatchet and picked up the plane to make the wood smooth and even, but as he drew it to and fro, he heard the same tiny voice.

This time poor Mastro Cherry fell as if shot. When he opened his eyes, he found himself sitting on the floor. In that very instant, a loud knock sounded on the door. "Come in," said the carpenter, not having an atom of strength left with which to stand up.

At the words, the door opened and a dapper little old man came in. His name was Geppetto.

"What brought you here, friend Geppetto?"

"I thought of making myself a beautiful wooden Marionette. It must be wonderful, one that will be able to dance, fence, and turn somersaults. With it I intend to go around the world, to earn

5

my crust of bread and cup of wine. What do you think of it?"

Mastro Antonio, very glad indeed, went immediately to his bench to get the piece of wood which had frightened him so much. Geppetto took the fine piece of wood, thanked Mastro Antonio, and limped away toward home.

"What brought you here, friend Geppetto?"

Little as Geppetto's house was, it was neat and comfortable. A fireplace full of burning logs was painted on the wall opposite the door. Over the fire, there was painted a pot full of something which kept boiling happily away and sending up clouds of what looked like real steam.

As soon as he reached home, Geppetto took his tools and

Geppetto began to cut and shape the wood into a Marionette.

began to cut and shape the wood into a Marionette. "What shall I call him?" he said to himself. "I think I'll call him Pinocchio. This name will make his fortune."

After choosing the name for his Marionette, Geppetto set seriously to work to make the hair, the forehead, the eyes. Fancy his surprise when he noticed that these eyes moved and then stared fixedly at him. Geppetto, seeing this, felt insulted and said in a grieved tone: "Ugly wooden eyes, why do you stare so?"

There was no answer. After the eyes, Geppetto made the nose, which began to stretch as soon as finished. It stretched and it S T R E T C H E D till it became so long it seemed endless.

Poor Geppetto kept cutting it and cutting it, but the more he cut, the longer grew that impertinent nose. In despair he left it alone.

Next he made the mouth. No sooner was it finished than it began to laugh and poke fun at him. "Stop laughing!" said Geppetto angrily; but he might as well have spoken to the wall.

"Stop laughing, I say!" he roared in a voice of thunder.

The mouth stopped laughing, but it stuck out a long tongue.

The legs and feet still had to be made. As soon as they were done, Geppetto felt a sharp kick on the tip of his nose.

"I deserve it!" he said to himself. "I should have thought of this before I made him. Now it's too late!"

Geppetto felt a sharp kick on the tip of his nose.

He took hold of the Marionette under the arms and put him on the floor to teach him to walk.

When his legs were limbered up, Pinocchio started walking by himself and ran all around the room. He came to the open door, and with one leap he was out into the street.

Away he flew! "Catch him! Catch him!" Geppetto kept shouting. But the people in the street, seeing a wooden Marionette running like the wind, stood still to stare and to laugh until they cried.

At last, by sheer luck, a Carabineer, a local policeman, came along. He grabbed the Marionette by the nose (it was an extremely long one and seemed made on purpose for that

9

Away he flew!

very thing) and returned him to Mastro Geppetto.

Geppetto shook him two or three times and said to him angrily: "We're going home now. When we get home, then we'll settle this matter!"

Pinocchio, on hearing this, threw himself on the ground and refused to take another step. One person after another gathered around the two.

Some said one thing, some another. They said so much that, finally, the Carabineer ended matters by setting Pinocchio at liberty and dragging Geppetto to prison.

The Carabineer dragged Geppetto to prison.

Geppetto in prison.

THE STORY
OF PINOCCHIO
& THE TALKING
CRICKET

IN WHICH ONE SEES THAT
BAD CHILDREN DO NOT LIKE
TO BE CORRECTED BY THOSE
WHO KNOW MORE
THAN THEY DO

CHAPTER TWO

PINOCCHIO, free now from the clutches of the Carabineer, was running wildly across fields and meadows, taking one short-cut after another toward home. On reaching home, he found the house door half-open.

He slipped into the room, locked the door, and threw himself on the floor, happy at his escape.

But his happiness lasted only a short time, for just then he heard someone saying: "Cri-ᶜʳⁱ-cri!"

"Who is calling me?" asked Pinocchio, greatly frightened.

"I am!"

Pinocchio turned and saw a large cricket crawling slowly up the wall.

"Tell me, Cricket, who are you?"

"I am the Talking Cricket and I have been living in this room

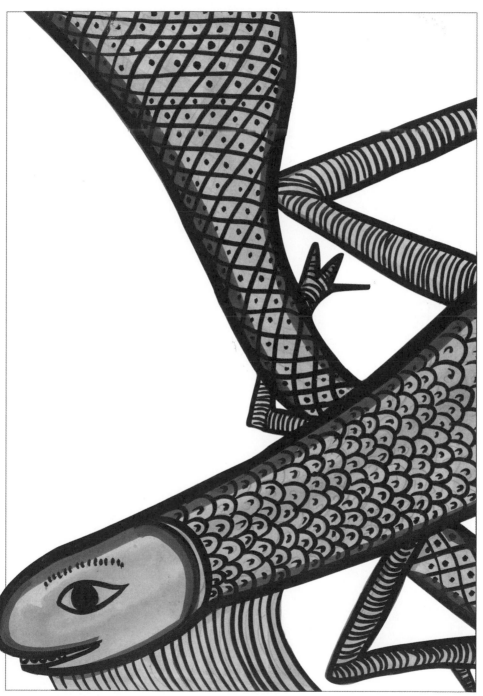

Pinocchio turned and saw a large cricket crawling slowly up the wall.

for more than one hundred years."

"Today, however, this room is mine," said the Marionette, "and if you wish to do me a favour, get out now, and don't turn around even once."

"I refuse to leave this spot," answered the Cricket, "until I have told you a great truth. Woe to boys who refuse to obey their parents and run away from home! They will never be happy in this world, and when they are older they will be very sorry for it."

"Sing on, Cricket mine, as you please. What I know is, that tomorrow, at dawn, I leave this place forever. If I stay here the same thing will happen to me which happens to all other boys and girls. They are sent to school, and whether they want to or not, they must study. As for me, let me tell you, I hate to study! It's much more fun, I think, to chase after butterflies, climb trees, and steal birds' nests."

But the Cricket, who was a wise old philosopher, instead of being offended at Pinocchio's impudence, continued in the same tone: "If you do not like going to school, why don't you at least learn a trade, so that you can earn an honest living?"

"Shall I tell you something?" asked Pinocchio, who was beginning to lose patience. "Of all the trades in the world, there is only one that really suits me. That of eating, drinking, sleeping, playing, and wandering around from morning till night."

"Let me tell you, for your own good, Pinocchio," said the Talking Cricket in his calm voice, "that those who follow that trade always end up in the hospital or in prison."

"Careful, ugly Cricket! If you make me angry, you'll be sorry!"

"Poor Pinocchio, I am sorry for you."

"Why?"

"Because you are a Marionette and, what is much worse, you have a wooden head."

At these last words, Pinocchio jumped up in a fury, took a hammer from the bench, and threw it with all his strength at the Talking Cricket.

Perhaps he did not think he would strike it. But, sad to relate,

Pinocchio threw a hammer at the Talking Cricket.

my dear children, he did hit the Cricket, straight on its head. With a last weak "cri-cri-cri" the poor Cricket fell from the wall, dead!

If the Cricket's death scared Pinocchio at all, it was only for a very few moments. For, as night came on, a queer, empty feeling at the pit of his stomach reminded the Marionette that he had eaten nothing as yet.

Poor Pinocchio ran to the fireplace where the pot was boiling and stretched out his hand to take the cover off, but to his amazement the pot was only painted! Think how he felt! His long nose became at least two inches longer. And meanwhile his hunger grew and grew.

Suddenly, he saw, among the sweepings in a corner, something round and white that looked very much like a hen's egg. In a jiffy he pounced upon it. It was an egg. The Marionette's joy knew no bounds. Certain that he was dreaming, he turned the egg over and over in his hands, fondled it, kissed it, and talked to it:

"And now, how shall I cook you? Shall I make an omelette? No, it is better to fry you in a pan! Or shall I drink you? No, the best way is to fry you in the pan. You will taste better."

No sooner said than done. He placed a little pan over a foot-warmer full of hot coals. In the pan, instead of oil or butter, he poured a little water. As soon as the water started to boil–tac!–

A little yellow Chick, fluffy and gay and smiling, escaped from the egg.

he broke the eggshell. But in place of the white and the yolk of the egg, a little yellow Chick, fluffy and gay and smiling, escaped from it. Bowing politely to Pinocchio, he said to him:

"Many, many thanks, indeed, Mr. Pinocchio, for having saved me the trouble of breaking my shell! Goodbye and good luck to you and remember me to the family!"

With these words he spread out his wings and, darting to the open window, he flew away into space till he was out of sight.

The poor Marionette stood as if turned to stone. His stomach kept grumbling more than ever and he had nothing to quiet it with. As he no longer had any strength left with which to stand, Pinocchio sat down on a little stool and put his two feet on the stove. There he fell asleep, and while he slept, his wooden feet began to burn.

Slowly, very slowly, they blackened and turned to ashes.

Pinocchio snored away happily as if his feet were not his own. At dawn he opened his eyes just as a loud knocking sounded at the door.

"Who is it?" he called, yawning and rubbing his eyes.

"It is I," answered a voice. "Open the door for me!"

"Father, dear Father, I can't," answered the Marionette in despair, crying and rolling on the floor.

"Why can't you?"

"Because someone has eaten my feet."

While Pinocchio slept, his wooden feet began to burn.

"And who has eaten them?"

"The cat," answered Pinocchio, seeing that little animal busily playing with some shavings in the corner of the room.

"Open! I say," repeated Geppetto, "or I'll give you a sound whipping when I get in."

"Father, believe me, I can't stand up. Oh, dear! Oh, dear! I shall have to walk on my knees all my life."

"Open, I say," repeated Geppetto.

GEPPETTO

MAKES

PINOCCHIO

a new pair of feet

AND SELLS HIS COAT
TO BUY HIM AN

A-B-C book

CHAPTER THREE

GEPPETTO, thinking that all these tears and cries were only other pranks of the Marionette, climbed up the side of the house and went in through the window. Geppetto felt sorry for Pinocchio, and pulling three pears out of his pocket, offered them to him, saying:

"These three pears were for my breakfast, but I give them to you gladly. Eat them and stop weeping."

The Marionette made a wry face, but, one after another, the skins and the cores disappeared. As soon as his hunger was appeased, the Marionette started to grumble and cry that he wanted a new pair of feet.

But Mastro Geppetto, in order to punish him for his mischief, left him alone the whole morning. After dinner he said to him: "Why should I make your feet over again? To see you run away from home once more?"

"I promise you," answered the Marionette, sobbing, "that from now on I'll be good."

Geppetto, though trying to look very stern, felt his eyes fill with tears and his heart soften when he saw Pinocchio so unhappy. He said no more, but taking his tools and two pieces of wood, he set to work diligently. In less than an hour the feet were finished, two slender, nimble little feet, strong and quick, modelled as if by an artist's hands. As soon as the Marionette felt his new feet, he gave one leap from the table and started to skip and jump around, as if he had lost his head from very joy.

"To show you how grateful I am to you, Father, I'll go to school

In less than an hour the feet were finished.

now. But to go to school I need a suit of clothes."

Geppetto did not have a penny in his pocket, so he made his son a little suit of flowered paper, a pair of shoes from the bark of a tree, and a tiny cap from a bit of dough. Pinocchio ran to look at himself in a bowl of water, and he felt so happy that he said proudly:

"Now I look like a gentleman but, in order to go to school, I still need something very important."

"What is it?"

"An A-B-C book."

Geppetto jumped up from his chair. Putting on his old coat, full of darns and patches, he ran out of the house without another word. After a while he returned. In his hands he had the A-B-C book for his son, but the old coat was gone. The poor fellow was in his shirt sleeves and the day was cold.

"Where's your coat, Father?"

"I have sold it."

"Why did you sell your coat?"

"It was too warm."

Pinocchio understood the answer in a twinkling, and, unable to restrain his tears, he jumped on his father's neck and kissed him over and over.

PINOCCHIO

sells his

A – **B** – **C** *book*

TO PAY HIS WAY
INTO THE

**MARIONETTE
THEATRE**

CHAPTER FOUR

SEE PINOCCHIO hurrying off to school with his new A-B-C book under his arm! As he walked along, he thought he heard sounds of pipes and drums coming from a distance: pi-pi-pi, pi-pi-pi, zum, zum, zum, zum.

He stopped to listen. Those sounds came from a little street that led to a small village along the shore.

"What can that noise be? What a nuisance that I have to go to school! Otherwise... Well, today I'll follow the pipes, and tomorrow I'll go to school. There's always plenty of time to go to school," decided the little rascal at last, shrugging his shoulders.

No sooner said than done. He started down the street, going like the wind. On he ran, and louder grew the sounds of pipe and drum: pi-pi-pi, pi-pi-pi, pi-pi-pi... zum-zum zum-zum-zum.

Suddenly, he found himself in a large square, full of people standing in front of a little wooden building painted in brilliant colours.

"What is that house?" Pinocchio asked a little boy near him.

"Read the sign and you'll know."

"I'd like to read, but somehow I can't today."

"Oh, really? Then I'll read it to you. Know, then, that written in letters of fire I see the words:

GREAT:MARIONETTE:THEATRE

"When did the show start?"

"It is starting now."

"And how much does one pay to get in?"

"Four pennies."

Pinocchio, who was wild with curiosity to know what was going on inside, lost all his pride and said to the boy shamelessly:

"For the price of four pennies, I'll sell you my coat."

"If it rains, what shall I do with a coat of flowered paper? I could not take it off again."

"Do you want to buy my shoes?"

"They are only good enough to light a fire with."

"What about my hat?"

"Fine bargain, indeed! A cap of dough! The mice might come

and eat it from my head!"

"I'll give you four pennies for your A-B-C book," said a ragpicker who stood by.

Then and there, the book changed hands. Quick as a flash, Pinocchio disappeared into the Marionette Theatre. And then something happened which almost caused a riot.

The curtain was up and the performance had started. Harlequin and Pulcinella were reciting on the stage and, as usual, they were threatening each other with sticks and blows. The play continued for a few minutes, and then suddenly, without any warning, Harlequin stopped talking. Turning toward the audience, he pointed to the rear of the orchestra, yelling wildly at the same time:

"Look, look! Am I asleep or awake? Or do I really see Pinocchio there?"

"It is Pinocchio! It is Pinocchio!" yelled all the Marionettes, pouring out of the wings. "It is Pinocchio. It is our brother Pinocchio! Hurrah for Pinocchio!"

"Pinocchio, come up to me!" shouted Harlequin. "Come to the arms of your wooden brothers!"

It is impossible to describe the shrieks of joy, the warm embraces, the knocks, and the friendly greetings with which that strange company of dramatic actors and actresses received Pinocchio.

It was a heart-rending spectacle, but the audience, seeing that the play had stopped, became angry and began to yell: "The play, the play, we want the play!"

The yelling was of no use, for the Marionettes, instead of going on with their act, made twice as much racket as before, and, lifting up Pinocchio on their shoulders, carried him around the stage in triumph.

At that very moment, the Director came out of his room. His mouth was as wide as an oven, his teeth like yellow fangs, and his eyes, two glowing red coals. In his huge, hairy hands, a long whip, made of green snakes and black cats' tails twisted together, swished through the air in a dangerous way.

"Why have you brought such excitement into my theatre;" the huge fellow asked Pinocchio with the voice of an ogre suffering with a cold.

"Believe me, your Honour, the fault was not mine."

"Enough! Be quiet! I'll take care of you later."

As soon as the play was over, the Director went to the kitchen, where a fine big lamb was slowly turning on the spit. More wood was needed to finish cooking it. He called Harlequin and Pulcinella and said to them:

"Bring that Marionette to me! He looks as if he were made of well-seasoned wood. He'll make a fine fire for this spit."

Harlequin and Pulcinella hesitated a bit. Then, frightened by a look from their master, they left the kitchen to obey him. A few minutes later they returned, carrying poor Pinocchio, who was wriggling and squirming like an eel and crying pitifully:

"Father, save me! I don't want to die! I don't want to die!"

"Father, save me!" cried Pinocchio.

FIRE EATER

SNEEZES

AND FORGIVES
PINOCCHIO,

WHO SAVES HIS
FRIEND, HARLEQUIN
FROM DEATH

CHAPTER FIVE

FIRE EATER (this was the Director's real name) was very ugly, but he was far from being as bad as he looked. Proof of this is that, when he saw the poor Marionette being brought in to him, struggling with fear and crying, "I don't want to die! I don't want to die!" he felt sorry for him and began first to waver and then to weaken. Finally, he could control himself no longer and gave a loud sneeze.

At that sneeze, Harlequin, who until then had been as sad as a weeping willow, smiled happily and leaning toward the Marionette, whispered to him:

"Good news, brother mine! Fire Eater has sneezed and this is a sign that he feels sorry for you. You are saved!"

For be it known, that, while other people, when sad and sorrowful, weep and wipe their eyes, Fire Eater, on the

"Stop crying! Your wails give me a funny feeling."

other hand, had the strange habit of sneezing each time he felt unhappy.

After sneezing, Fire Eater, ugly as ever, cried to Pinocchio: "Stop crying! Your wails give me a funny feeling down here in my stomach and–E–tchee!–E–tchee*e!*" Two loud sneezes finished his speech.

"God bless you!" said Pinocchio.

"Thanks! Are your father and mother still living?" demanded Fire Eater.

"My father, yes. My mother I have never known."

"Your poor father would suffer terribly if I were to use you as firewood. Poor old man! I feel sorry for him! E–tchee*!*

E–$t$chee$_e$! E–tchhee!" Three more sneezes sounded, louder than ever.

"God bless you!" said Pinocchio.

"Thanks! However, I ought to be sorry for myself, too, just now. My good dinner is spoiled. I have no more wood for the fire, and the lamb is only half-cooked. Never mind! In your place I'll burn some other Marionette. Hey there! Officers! Take Harlequin, tie him, and throw him on the fire. I want my lamb well done!"

Think how poor Harlequin felt! He was so scared that his legs doubled up under him and he fell to the floor. Pinocchio, at that heartbreaking sight, threw himself at the feet of Fire Eater and, weeping bitterly, asked in a pitiful voice which could scarcely be heard:

"Have pity, I beg of you, Signore!"

"There are no Signori here!"

"Have pity, kind Sir!"

"There are no Sirs here!"

"Have pity, your Excellency!"

On hearing himself addressed as your Excellency, the Director of the Marionette Theater smiled proudly as he said to Pinocchio:

"Well, what do you want from me now, Marionette?"

"I beg for mercy for my poor friend, Harlequin, who has never

"Take Harlequin, tie him, and throw him on the fire."

done the least harm in his life."

"There is no mercy here, Pinocchio. I have spared you. Harlequin must burn in your place. I am hungry and my dinner must be cooked."

"In that case, my duty is clear. Come, officers! Tie me up and throw me on those flames!"

These brave words, said in a piercing voice, made all the other Marionettes cry.

Fire Eater at first remained hard and cold as a piece of ice; but then, little by little, he softened and began to sneeze. And after four or five sneezes, he opened wide his arms and said to Pinocchio:

"You are a brave boy! Come to my arms and kiss me!"

"Has pardon been granted to me?" asked poor Harlequin with a voice that was hardly a breath.

"Pardon is yours!" answered Fire Eater, sighing and wagging his head.

At the news that pardon had been given, the Marionettes ran to the stage and, turning on all the lights, they danced and sang till dawn.

Fire Eater

GIVES PINOCCHIO FIVE GOLD PIECES FOR GEPPETTO

BUT THE MARIONETTE MEETS A FOX AND A CAT AND FOLLOWS THEM

CHAPTER SIX

THE NEXT DAY, FIRE EATER called Pinocchio aside and asked him:

"What is your father's name?"

"Geppetto."

"And what is his trade?"

"He's a wood carver."

"Does he earn much?"

"He earns so much that he never has a penny in his pockets. Just think that, in order to buy me an A-B-C book for school, he had to sell the only coat he owned, a coat so full of darns and patches that it was a pity."

"Poor fellow! I feel sorry for him. Here, take these five gold pieces. Go, give them to him with my kindest regards."

Pinocchio, as may easily be imagined, thanked him a

"Here, take these five gold pieces."

thousand times. He kissed each Marionette in turn, even the officers, and, beside himself with joy, set out on his homeward journey.

He had gone barely half a mile when he met a lame Fox and a blind Cat, walking together like two good friends.

"Good morning, Pinocchio," said the Fox, greeting him courteously.

"How do you know my name?" asked the Marionette.

"I know your father well. I saw him yesterday standing at the door of his house."

"And what was he doing?"

"He was in his shirt sleeves trembling with cold."

41

"Poor Father! But, after today, God willing, he will suffer no longer."

"Why?"

"Because I have become a rich man."

"You, a rich man?" said the Fox, and he began to laugh out loud. The Cat was laughing also, but tried to hide it by stroking his long whiskers.

"There is nothing to laugh at," cried Pinocchio angrily. And he pulled out the gold pieces which Fire Eater had given him.

At the cheerful tinkle of the gold, the Fox unconsciously held out his paw that was supposed to be lame, and the Cat opened wide his two eyes till they looked like live coals, but he closed them again so quickly that Pinocchio did not notice.

"And may I ask," inquired the Fox, "what you are going to do with all that money?"

"First of all," answered the Marionette, "I want to buy a fine new coat for my father, a coat of gold and silver with diamond buttons; after that, I'll buy an A-B-C book for myself. I want to go to school and study hard."

"Look at me," said the Fox. "For the silly reason of wanting to study, I have lost a paw."

"Look at me," said the Cat. "For the same foolish reason, I have lost the sight of both eyes."

At that moment, a Blackbird, perched on the fence along the

"Come with us, to the City of Simple Simons," said the Fox and the Cat.

road, called out sharp and clear:

"Pinocchio, do not listen to bad advice. If you do, you'll be sorry!" Poor little Blackbird! If he had only kept his words to himself! In the twinkling of an eyelid, the Cat leapt on him, and ate him, feathers and all. After eating the bird, he cleaned his whiskers, closed his eyes, and became blind once more.

"Poor Blackbird!" said Pinocchio to the Cat. "Why did you kill him?"

"I killed him to teach him a lesson. He talks too much. Next time he will keep his words to himself."

By this time the three companions had walked a long distance. Suddenly, the Fox stopped in his tracks and, turning to the Marionette, said to him:

"Do you want to double your gold pieces? Do you want one hundred, a thousand, two thousand gold pieces for your miserable five?"

"Yes, but how?"

"The way is very easy. Instead of returning home, come with us. To the City of Simple Simons."

Pinocchio thought a while and then said firmly: "No, I don't want to go. Home is near, and I'm going where Father is waiting for me. How unhappy he must be that I have not yet returned! I have been a bad son, and the Talking Cricket was right when he said that a disobedient boy cannot be happy in this world. I have learnt this at my own expense."

"Well, then," said the Fox, "if you really want to go home, go ahead, but you'll be sorry. Think well, Pinocchio, you are turning your back on Dame Fortune."

"On Dame Fortune," repeated the Cat.

"Tomorrow your five gold pieces will be two thousand!"

"But how can they possibly become so many?" asked Pinocchio wonderingly.

"I'll explain," said the Fox. "You must know that, just outside the City of Simple Simons, there is a blessed field called the Field of Wonders. In this field you dig a hole and in the hole you bury a gold piece. After covering up the hole with earth

Poor little Blackbird!

you water it well, sprinkle a bit of salt on it, and go to bed. During the night, the gold piece sprouts, grows, blossoms, and next morning you find a beautiful tree that is loaded with gold pieces."

"So that if I were to bury my five gold pieces," cried Pinocchio with growing wonder, "next morning I should find—how many?"

"It is very simple to figure out," answered the Fox. "Why, you can figure it on your fingers! Granted that each piece gives you five hundred, multiply five hundred by five. Next morning you will find twenty-five hundred new, sparkling gold pieces."

"Fine! Fine!" cried Pinocchio, dancing about with joy. "And as soon as I have them, I shall keep two thousand for myself and the other five hundred I'll give to you two."

"A gift for us?" cried the Fox, pretending to be insulted. "Why, of course not! We do not work for gain," answered the Fox. "We work only to enrich others."

"What good people," thought Pinocchio to himself. And forgetting his father, the new coat, the A-B-C book, and all his good resolutions, he said to the Fox and to the Cat:

"Let us go. I am with you."

THE INN OF THE
RED
LOBSTER

CHAPTER SEVEN

CAT AND FOX AND MARIONETTE walked and walked and walked. At last, toward evening, dead tired, they came to the Inn of the Red Lobster.

"Let us stop here a while," said the Fox, "to eat a bite and rest for a few hours. At midnight we'll start out again, for at dawn tomorrow we must be at the Field of Wonders."

Supper over, Pinocchio, the Fox and Cat went to bed. As soon as he was in bed, Pinocchio fell asleep and began to dream. He dreamt he was in the middle of a field. The field was full of vines heavy with grapes. The grapes were no other than gold coins which tinkled merrily as they swayed in the wind. They seemed to say, "Let him who wants us take us!"

Just as Pinocchio stretched out his hand to take a handful of them, he was awakened by three loud knocks at the door. It was the Innkeeper who had come to tell him that midnight had struck.

"Are my friends ready?" the Marionette asked him.

"Indeed, yes! They went two hours ago."

"Why in such a hurry?"

"Unfortunately the Cat received a telegram which said that his first-born was suffering from chilblains and was on the point of death. He could not even wait to say goodbye to you."

"Did they pay for the supper?"

"How could they do such a thing? Being people of great refinement, they did not want to offend you so deeply as not to allow you the honour of paying the bill."

"Too bad! That offence would have been more than pleasing to me," said Pinocchio, scratching his head. "Where did my good friends say they would wait for me?" he added.

"At the Field of Wonders, at sunrise tomorrow morning."

Pinocchio paid a gold piece for the three suppers and started on his way toward the field that was to make him a rich man. He walked on, not knowing where he was going, for it was dark, so dark that not a thing was visible. Round about him, not a leaf stirred. A few bats skimmed his nose now and again and scared him half to death.

As he walked, Pinocchio noticed a tiny insect glimmering on the trunk of a tree, a small being that glowed with a pale, soft light.

"Who are you?" he asked.

"I am the ghost of the Talking Cricket," answered the little being in a faint voice that sounded as if it came from a far away world.

"What do you want?" asked the Marionette.

"I want to give you a few words of good advice. Don't listen to those who promise you wealth overnight, my boy. As a rule they are either fools or swindlers! Listen to me and go home."

"But I want to go on!"

"The hour is late!"

"I want to go on."

"The night is very dark."

"I want to go on."

"The road is dangerous."

"I want to go on."

"Remember that boys who insist on having their own way, sooner or later come to grief."

"The same nonsense. Goodbye, Cricket."

"Good night, Pinocchio, and may Heaven preserve you from the Assassins."

"I am the ghost of the Talking Cricket," answered the little being.

"The same nonsense. Goodbye, Cricket."

PINOCCHIO

[NOT HAVING LISTENED
TO THE GOOD ADVICE OF
THE TALKING CRICKET]

*Falls into the Hands
of the Assassins*

CHAPTER EIGHT

"DEAR, OH, DEAR! When I come to think of it," said the Marionette to himself, as he once more set out on his journey, "we boys are really very unlucky. Everybody scolds us, everybody gives us advice, everybody warns us. If we were to allow it, everyone would try to be father and mother to us; everyone, even the Talking Cricket. Take me, for example. Just because I would not listen to that bothersome Cricket, who knows how many misfortunes may be awaiting me! Assassins indeed! At least I have never believed in them, nor ever will. To speak sensibly, I think assassins have been invented by fathers and mothers to frighten children who want to run away at night."

Pinocchio was not given time to argue any longer, for he thought he heard a slight rustle among the leaves behind him. He turned to look and behold, there in the darkness stood two

In the darkness stood two black shadows.

big black shadows, wrapped from head to foot in black sacks. The two figures leapt toward him as softly as if they were ghosts.

"Here they come!" Pinocchio said to himself, and, not knowing where to hide the gold pieces, he stuck all four of them under his tongue.

He tried to run away, but hardly had he taken a step, when he felt his arms grasped and heard two horrible, deep voices say to him: "Your money or your life!"

On account of the gold pieces in his mouth, Pinocchio could not say a word, so he tried with head and hands and body to show, as best he could, that he was only a poor Marionette without a penny in his pocket.

"Out with that money or you're a dead man," said the taller of the two Assassins.

"Dead man," repeated the other.

"And after having killed you, we will kill your father also."

"Your father also!"

"No, no, no, not my Father!" cried Pinocchio, wild with terror; but as he screamed, the gold pieces tinkled together in his mouth.

"Ah, you rascal! So that's the game! You have the money hidden under your tongue. Out with it!"

But Pinocchio was as stubborn as ever.

One of them grabbed the Marionette by the nose and the other by the chin, and they pulled him unmercifully from side to side in order to make him open his mouth.

All was of no use. The Marionette's lips might have been nailed together. They would not open. In desperation the smaller of the two Assassins pulled out a long knife from his pocket, and tried to pry Pinocchio's mouth open with it.

Quick as a flash, the Marionette sank his teeth deep into the Assassin's hand, bit it off and spat it out. Fancy his surprise when he saw that it was not a hand, but a cat's paw.

Encouraged by this first victory, he freed himself from the claws of his assailers and, leaping over the bushes along the road, ran swiftly across the fields. His pursuers were after him at once, like two dogs chasing a hare. As he ran, the Marionette felt more and more certain that he would have to give himself up into the hands of his pursuers. Suddenly he saw a little cottage gleaming white as the snow among the trees of the forest.

After a hard race of almost an hour, tired and out of breath, Pinocchio finally reached the door of the cottage and knocked. No one answered. He knocked again, harder than before, for behind him he heard the steps and the laboured breathing of his persecutors. The same silence followed. As knocking was of no use, Pinocchio, in despair, began to kick and bang against the door, as if he wanted to break it. At the noise, a window opened and a lovely maiden looked out. She had azure hair and a face white as wax. Her eyes were closed and her hands crossed on her breast. With a voice so weak that it hardly could be heard, she whispered:

"No one lives in this house. Everyone is dead."

"Won't you, at least, open the door for me?" cried Pinocchio in a beseeching voice.

"I also am dead."

"Dead? What are you doing at the window, then?"

"I am waiting for the coffin to take me away."

After these words, the little girl disappeared and the window closed without a sound.

"Oh, Lovely Maiden with Azure Hair," cried Pinocchio, "open,

A lovely maiden with azure hair looked out.

I beg of you. Take pity on a poor boy who is being chased by two Assass*s*—"

He did not finish, for two powerful hands grasped him by the neck and the same two horrible voices growled threateningly: "Now we have you!" The Marionette, seeing death dancing before him, trembled so hard that the joints of his legs rattled and the coins tinkled under his tongue.

"Well," the Assassins asked, "will you open your mouth now or not? Ah! You do not answer? Very well, this time you shall open it."

Taking out two long, sharp knives, they struck two heavy blows on the Marionette's back. Happily for him, Pinocchio was made of very hard wood and the knives broke into a thousand pieces. The Assassins looked at each other in dismay, holding the handles of the knives in their hands.

"I understand," said one of them to the other, "there is nothing left to do now but to hang him."

"To hang him," repeated the other.

Throwing the rope over the high limb of a giant oak tree, they pulled till the poor Marionette hung far up in space.

Satisfied with their work, they sat on the grass waiting for Pinocchio to give his last gasp. But after three hours the Marionette's eyes were still open and his mouth still shut.

Tired of waiting, the Assassins called to him mockingly: "Goodbye till tomorrow. When we return in the morning, we hope you'll be polite enough to let us find you dead and gone and with your mouth wide open." With these words they went.

Death was creeping nearer and nearer, and the Marionette still hoped for some good soul to come to his rescue, but no one appeared. These were his last words. He closed his eyes, opened his mouth, stretched out his legs, and hung there, as if he were dead.

The Assassins called to him mockingly: "Goodbye until tomorrow."

The Lovely Maiden
with Azure Hair

SENDS FOR THE
POOR MARIONETTE,
PUTS HIM TO BED
& CALLS THREE DOCTORS

AFTERWARDS HE TELLS A
LIE AND HIS NOSE GROWS

CHAPTER NINE

IF THE POOR MARIONETTE had dangled there much longer, all hope would have been lost. Luckily for him, the Lovely Maiden with Azure Hair once again looked out of her window. Filled with pity at the sight of the poor little fellow being knocked helplessly about by the wind, she clapped her hands sharply together three times.

At the signal, a loud whirr of wings in quick flight was heard and a large Falcon came and settled itself on the window ledge.

"What do you command, my charming Fairy?" asked the Falcon, bending his beak in deep reverence (for it must be known that, after all, the Lovely Maiden with Azure Hair was none other than a very kind Fairy who had lived, for more than a thousand years, in the vicinity of the forest.)

"Do you see that Marionette hanging from the limb of that

A large Falcon came and settled itself on the window ledge.

giant oak tree? Fly immediately to him. With your strong beak, break the knot which holds him tied, take him down, and lay him softly on the grass at the foot of the oak."

The Falcon flew away and after two minutes returned, saying, "I have done what you have commanded."

The Fairy clapped her hands twice. A magnificent Poodle appeared, walking on his hind legs just like a man.

"Come, Medoro," said the Fairy to him. "Get my best coach ready and set out toward the forest. On reaching the oak tree, you will find a poor, half-dead Marionette stretched out on the grass. Lift him up tenderly, place him on the silken cushions of the coach, and bring him here to me."

In a few minutes, a lovely little coach, made of glass, with lining as soft as whipped cream and chocolate pudding, and stuffed with canary feathers, pulled out of the stable. It was drawn by one hundred pairs of white mice, and the Poodle sat on the coachman's seat and snapped his whip gayly in the air, as if he were a real coachman in a hurry to get to his destination.

In a quarter of an hour the coach was back. The Fairy, who was waiting at the door of the house, lifted the poor little Marionette in her arms, took him to a dainty room with mother-of-pearl walls and put him to bed. Touching him on the forehead, she noticed that he was burning with fever.

She took a glass of water, put a white powder into it, and,

A lovely little coach pulled out of the stable.

handing it to the Marionette, said lovingly to him:

"Drink this, and in a few days you'll be up and well."

Pinocchio looked at the glass, made a wry face, and asked in a whining voice: "Is it sweet or bitter?"

"It is bitter, but it is good for you."

"If it is bitter, I don't want it."

"Drink it and I'll give you a lump of sugar to take the bitter taste from your mouth."

"Where's the sugar?"

"Here it is," said the Fairy, taking a lump from a golden sugar bowl.

"I want the sugar first, then I'll drink the bitter water."

The Fairy gave him the sugar and Pinocchio, after chewing and swallowing it in a twinkling, said, smacking his lips:

"If only sugar were medicine! I should take it every day."

"Now keep your promise and drink these few drops of water. They'll be good for you."

Pinocchio took the glass in both hands and stuck his nose into it. He lifted it to his mouth and once more stuck his nose into it.

"I won't drink it," cried Pinocchio, bursting out crying. "I won't drink this awful water. I won't. I won't! No, no, no, no!"

"My boy, you'll be sorry. In a few hours the fever will take you far away to another world."

"I don't care."

"Aren't you afraid of death?"

"Not a bit. I'd rather die than drink that awful medicine."

At that moment, the door of the room flew open and in came four Rabbits as black as ink, carrying a small black coffin on their shoulders.

"What do you want from me?" asked Pinocchio.

"We have come for you," said the largest Rabbit.

"For me? But I'm not dead yet!"

"No, not dead yet; but you will be in a few moments since you have refused to take the medicine which would have made you well."

"Oh, Fairy, my Fairy," the Marionette cried out, "give me that glass! Quick, please! I don't want to die! No, no, not yet–not yet!"

And holding the glass with his two hands, he swallowed the medicine at one gulp.

"Well," said the four Rabbits, "this time we have made the trip for nothing."

And turning on their heels, they marched solemnly out of the room, carrying their little black coffin and muttering and grumbling between their teeth.

In a twinkling, Pinocchio felt fine.

"Come here now and tell me how it came about that you found yourself in the hands of the Assassins."

And so he told her the story of the Assassins and the gold coins.

"Where are the gold pieces now?" the Fairy asked.

"I lost them," answered Pinocchio, but he told a lie, for he had them in his pocket.

As he spoke, his nose, long though it was, became at least two inches longer.

"And where did you lose them?"

"In the wood nearby."

At this second lie, his nose grew a few more inches.

"If you lost them in the nearby wood," said the Fairy, "we'll look for them and find them, for everything that is lost there is always found."

"Ah, now I remember," replied the Marionette, becoming more and more confused. "I did not lose the gold pieces, but I swallowed them when I drank the medicine."

At this third lie, his nose became longer than ever, so long that he could not even turn around. If he turned to the right, he knocked it against the bed or into the windowpanes; if he turned to the left, he struck the walls or the door; if he raised it a bit, he almost put the Fairy's eyes out.

The Fairy sat looking at him and laughing.

"Why do you laugh?" the Marionette asked her, worried now at the sight of his growing nose.

"I am laughing at your lies."

"How do you know I am lying?"

"Lies, my boy, are known in a moment. There are two kinds of lies, lies with short legs and lies with long noses. Yours, just now, happen to have long noses."

Crying as if his heart would break, the Marionette mourned for hours over the length of his nose. No matter how he tried, it would not go through the door. The Fairy showed no pity toward him, as she was trying to teach him a good lesson, so that he would stop telling lies, the worst habit any boy may acquire.

But when she saw him, pale with fright and with his eyes half out of his head from terror, she began to feel sorry for him and clapped her hands together. A thousand woodpeckers flew in through the window and settled themselves on Pinocchio's nose. They pecked and pecked so hard at that enormous nose that in a few moments, it was the same size as before.

A thousand woodpeckers settled themselves on Pinocchio's nose.

Pinocchio

FINDS THE **FOX**
AND THE **CAT** AGAIN,
AND GOES WITH THEM
TO SOW THE **GOLD
PIECES** IN

the Field of Wonders

CHAPTER TEN

"HOW GOOD YOU ARE, MY FAIRY," said Pinocchio, drying his eyes, "and how much I love you!"

"I love you, too," answered the Fairy, "and if you wish to stay with me, you may be my little brother and I'll be your good little sister."

"I should like to stay—but what about my poor father?"

"I have thought of everything. Your father has been sent for and before night he will be here."

"Really?" cried Pinocchio joyfully. "Then, my good Fairy, if you are willing, I should like to go to meet him. I cannot wait to kiss that dear old man, who has suffered so much for my sake."

Pinocchio set out, and as soon as he found himself in the wood, he ran like a hare. When he reached the giant oak tree he stopped, for he thought he heard a rustle in the brush. He was right. There stood the Fox and the Cat, the two travelling companions with whom he had eaten at the Inn of the Red Lobster.

"Here comes our dear Pinocchio!" cried the Fox, hugging and kissing him.

"How did you happen here?"

"It is a long story," said the Marionette. "Let me tell it to you…" As he told the story, Pinocchio noticed that the Cat carried his right paw in a sling.

"What happened to your paw?" he asked.

The Cat tried to answer, but he became so terribly twisted in his speech that the Fox had to help him out.

"My friend is too modest to answer. I'll answer for him. About an hour ago, we met an old wolf on the road. He was half-starved and begged for help. Having nothing to give him, what do you think my friend did out of the kindness of his heart? With his teeth, he bit off the paw of his front foot and threw it at that poor beast, so that he might have something to eat."

As he spoke, the Fox wiped off a tear. Pinocchio, almost in tears himself, whispered in the Cat's ear: "If all the cats were like you, how lucky the mice would be!"

"And what are you doing here?" the Fox asked the Marionette.

"I am waiting for my father, who will be here at any moment now."

The cat became so terribly twisted in his speech.

"And your gold pieces?"

"I still have them in my pocket, except one which I spent at the Inn of the Red Lobster."

"To think that those four gold pieces might become two thousand tomorrow. Why don't you listen to me? Why don't you sow them in the Field of Wonders?"

"Today it is impossible. I'll go with you some other time."

"Another day will be too late," said the Fox.

"Why?"

"Because that field has been bought by a very rich man, and today is the last day that it will be open to the public."

"How far is this Field of Wonders?"

"Only two miles away. Will you come with us? We'll be there in half an hour. You can sow the money, and, after a few minutes, you will gather your two thousand coins and return home rich. Are you coming?"

Pinocchio hesitated a moment before answering, for he remembered the good Fairy, old Geppetto, and the advice of the Talking Cricket. Then he ended by doing what all boys do, when they have no heart and little brain. He shrugged his shoulders and said to the Fox and the Cat:

"Let us go! I am with you."

They walked and walked for a half a day at least and at last they came to the town called the City of Simple Simons. As soon as they entered the town, Pinocchio noticed that all the streets were filled with hairless dogs, yawning from hunger; with sheared sheep, trembling with cold; with combless chickens, begging for a grain of wheat; with large butterflies, unable to use their wings because they had sold all their lovely colours; with tail-less peacocks, ashamed to show themselves; and with bedraggled pheasants, scuttling away hurriedly, grieving for their bright feathers of gold and silver, lost to them forever.

"Where is the Field of Wonders?" asked Pinocchio, growing tired of waiting.

"Be patient. It is only a few more steps away."

They passed through the city and, just outside the walls, they stepped into a lonely field, which looked more or less like any other field.

"Here we are," said the Fox to the Marionette. "Dig a hole here and put the gold pieces into it."

The Marionette obeyed. He dug the hole, put the four gold pieces into it, and covered them up very carefully. "Now," said the Fox, "go to that nearby brook, bring back a pail full of water, and sprinkle it over the spot."

Pinocchio followed the directions closely, but, as he had no pail, he pulled off his shoe, filled it with water, and sprinkled the earth which covered the gold. Then he asked:

"Anything else?"

"Where is the Field of Wonders?" asked Pinocchio, tired of waiting.

"Nothing else," answered the Fox. "Now we can go. Return here within twenty minutes and you will find the vine grown and the branches filled with gold pieces."

Pinocchio, beside himself with joy, thanked the Fox and the Cat many times and promised them each a beautiful gift.

They said goodbye to Pinocchio and, wishing him good luck, went on their way.

Pinocchio followed the directions and sprinkled the earth.

PINOCCHIO
is robbed of his
gold pieces and,
in punishment,
is sentenced to
four months in
| PRISON |

CHAPTER ELEVEN

IF THE MARIONETTE had been told to wait a day instead of twenty minutes, the time could not have seemed longer to him. He walked impatiently to and fro and finally turned his nose toward the Field of Wonders.

Twenty minutes later, he came to the field. There he stopped to see if, by any chance, a vine filled with gold coins was in sight. But he saw nothing! He took a few steps forward, and still nothing! He stepped into the field. He went up to the place where he had dug the hole and buried the gold pieces. Again nothing! Pinocchio became very thoughtful and, forgetting his good manners altogether, he pulled a hand out of his pocket and gave his head a thorough scratching.

As he did so, he heard a hearty burst of laughter close to his head. He turned sharply, and there, just above him on the branch of a tree, sat a large Parrot, busily preening his feathers.

"What are you laughing at?" Pinocchio asked peevishly.

"I am laughing at those simpletons who believe everything they hear and who allow themselves to be caught so easily in the traps set for them."

"Do you, perhaps, mean me?"

"I certainly do mean you, poor Pinocchio—you who are such a little silly as to believe that gold can be sown in a field just like beans or squash."

"I don't know what you are talking about," said the Marionette, who was beginning to tremble with fear.

"Too bad! I'll explain myself better," said the Parrot. "While you were away in the city the Fox and the Cat returned here in a great hurry. They took the four gold pieces which you have buried and ran away as fast as the wind. If you can catch them, you're a brave one!"

Pinocchio's mouth opened wide. He would not believe the Parrot's words and began to dig away furiously at the earth. He dug and he dug till the hole was as big as himself, but no money was there. Every penny was gone.

In desperation, he ran to the city and went straight to the courthouse to report the robbery to the magistrate. The Judge was a Monkey, a large Gorilla venerable with age. A flowing white beard covered his chest and he wore gold-rimmed spectacles from which the glasses had dropped out. The reason for wearing these, he said, was that his eyes had been weakened by the work of many years.

Pinocchio, standing before him, told his pitiful tale, word by word. He gave the names and the descriptions of the robbers and begged for justice.

The Judge listened to him with great patience. A kind look shone in his eyes. He became very much interested in the story; he felt moved; he almost wept. When the Marionette had no more to say, the Judge put out his hand and rang a bell.

At the sound, two large Mastiffs appeared, dressed in Carabineers' uniforms.

Then the magistrate, pointing to Pinocchio, said in a very solemn voice:

"This poor simpleton has been robbed of four gold pieces. Take him, therefore, and throw him into prison." The Marionette, on hearing this sentence passed upon him, was thoroughly stunned. He tried to protest, but the two officers clapped their paws on his mouth and hustled him away to jail.

There he had to remain for four long, weary months. And if it had not been for a very lucky chance, he probably would have had to stay there longer. For, my dear children, you must know that it happened just then that the young Emperor who ruled over the City of Simple Simons had gained a great victory over his enemy, and in celebration thereof, he had ordered illuminations, fireworks, shows of all kinds, and, best of all, the opening of all prison doors.

"If the others go, I go, too," said Pinocchio to the Jailer.

"In that case you also are free," said the Jailer. Taking off his cap, he bowed low and opened the door of the prison, and Pinocchio ran out and away, with never a look backward.

Fancy the happiness of Pinocchio on finding himself free! Without saying yes or no, he fled from the city and set out on the road that was to take him back to the house of the lovely Fairy.

He stopped suddenly, frozen with terror. What was the matter? An immense Serpent lay stretched across the road—a Serpent with a bright green skin, fiery eyes which glowed and burned, and a pointed tail that smoked like a chimney.

How frightened was poor Pinocchio! Pinocchio, trying to feel very brave, walked straight up to him and said in a sweet, soothing voice: "I beg your pardon, Mr. Serpent, would you be so kind as to step aside to let me pass?"

He might as well have talked to a wall. The Serpent never moved. Once more, in the same sweet voice, he spoke:

"You must know, Mr. Serpent, that I am going home where my father is waiting for me. It is so long since I have seen him! Would you mind very much if I passed?"

He waited for some sign of an answer to his questions, but

The serpent shot up like a spring.

the answer did not come.

"Is he dead, I wonder?" said Pinocchio, rubbing his hands together happily. Without a moment's hesitation, he started to step over him, but he had just raised one leg when the Serpent shot up like a spring and the Marionette fell head over heels backward. He fell so awkwardly that his head stuck in the mud, and there he stood with his legs straight up in the air.

At the sight of the Marionette kicking and squirming like a young whirlwind, the Serpent laughed so heartily and so long that at last he burst an artery and died on the spot. Pinocchio freed himself from his awkward position and once more began to run in order to reach the Fairy's house before dark. As he went, the pangs of hunger grew so strong that, unable to withstand them, he jumped into a field to pick a few grapes that tempted him. Woe to him!

No sooner had he reached the grapevine than—crack! went his legs. The poor Marionette was caught in a trap set there by a Farmer for some Weasels which came every night to steal his chickens.

The poor Marionette was caught in a trap.

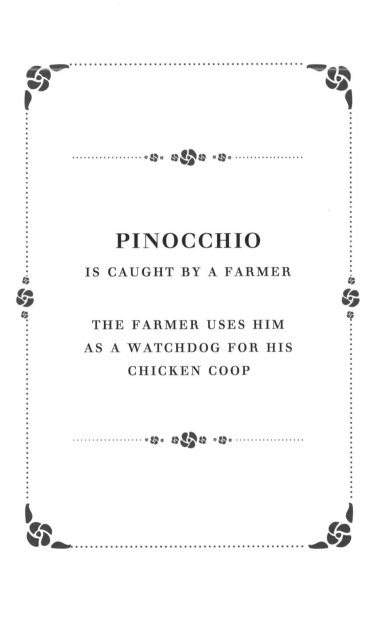

PINOCCHIO

IS CAUGHT BY A FARMER

THE FARMER USES HIM
AS A WATCHDOG FOR HIS
CHICKEN COOP

CHAPTER TWELVE

PINOCCHIO, as you may well imagine, began to scream and weep and beg; but all was of no use, for no houses were to be seen and not a soul passed by on the road.

Night came on. A little because of the sharp pain in his legs, a little because of fright at finding himself alone in the darkness of the field, the Marionette was about to faint, when he saw a tiny Glow-worm flickering by. He called to her and said:

"Dear little Glow-worm, will you set me free?"

"Poor little fellow!" replied the Glow-worm, stopping to look at him with pity. "How came you to be caught in this trap?"

"I stepped into this lonely field to take a few grapes and–"

"Are the grapes yours?"

"No."

"Who has taught you to take things that don't belong to you?"

"I was hungry."

"Hunger, my boy, is no reason for taking something which belongs to another."

"It's true, it's true!" cried Pinocchio in tears. "I won't do it again."

Just then, the conversation was interrupted by approaching footsteps. It was the owner of the field, who was coming on tiptoes to see if, by chance, he had caught the Weasels which had been eating his chickens.

Great was his surprise when, on holding up his lantern, he saw that, instead of a Weasel, he had caught a boy!

"Ah, you little thief!" said the Farmer in an angry voice. "So you are the one who steals my chickens!"

"Not I! No, no!" cried Pinocchio, sobbing bitterly. "I came here only to take a very few grapes."

"He who steals grapes may very easily steal chickens also. Take my word for it, I'll give you a lesson that you'll remember for a long while."

He opened the trap, grabbed the Marionette by the collar, and carried him to the house as if he were a puppy.

"It is late now and it's time for bed. Tomorrow we'll settle matters. In the meantime, since my watchdog died today, you may take his place and guard my henhouse."

No sooner said than done. He slipped a dog collar around

Pinocchio's neck and tightened it so that it would not come off. A long iron chain was tied to the collar. The other end of the chain was nailed to the wall.

"If tonight it should happen to rain," said the Farmer, "you can sleep in that little doghouse nearby, where you will find plenty of straw for a soft bed. It has been Melampo's bed for three years, and it will be good enough for you. And if, by any chance, any thieves should come, be sure to bark!"

After this last warning, the Farmer went into the house and closed the door and barred it.

Poor Pinocchio huddled close to the doghouse more dead than alive from cold, hunger, and fright. Now and again he pulled and tugged at the collar which nearly choked him. At last he went into the doghouse and fell asleep.

The Marionette slept on peacefully for a few hours till well along toward midnight, when he was awakened by strange whisperings and stealthy sounds coming from the yard. He stuck his nose out of the doghouse and saw four slender, hairy animals. They were Weasels, small animals very fond of both eggs and chickens.

One of them left her companions and, going to the door of the doghouse, said in a sweet voice:

"Good evening, Melampo."

"My name is not Melampo," answered Pinocchio.

He stuck his nose out and saw four slender animals.

"Who are you, then?"

"I am Pinocchio."

"What are you doing here?"

"I'm the watchdog."

"But where is Melampo? Where is the old dog who used to live in this house?"

"He died this morning."

"Died? Poor beast! He was so good! Still, judging by your face, I think you, too, are a good-natured dog."

"I beg your pardon, I am not a dog!"

"What are you, then?"

"I am a Marionette."

"Are you taking the place of the watchdog?"

"I'm sorry to say that I am. I'm being punished."

"Well, I shall make the same terms with you that we had with the dead Melampo. I am sure you will be glad to hear them."

"And what are the terms?"

"This is our plan: We'll come once in a while, as in the past, to pay a visit to this henhouse, and we'll take away eight chickens. Of these, seven are for us, and one for you, provided, of course, that you will make believe you are sleeping and will not bark for the Farmer."

"Did Melampo really do that?" asked Pinocchio.

"Indeed he did, and because of that we were the best of friends. Sleep away peacefully, and remember that before we go we shall leave you a nice fat chicken all ready for your breakfast in the morning. Is that understood?"

"Even too well," answered Pinocchio. And shaking his head in a threatening manner, he seemed to say, "We'll talk this over in a few minutes, my friends."

As soon as the four Weasels had talked things over, they went straight to the chicken coop which stood close to the doghouse. Digging busily with teeth and claws, they opened the little door and slipped in. But they were no sooner in than they heard the door close with a sharp bang.

The one who had done the trick was Pinocchio, who, not

satisfied with that, dragged a heavy stone in front of it. That done, he started to bark. And he barked as if he were a real watchdog: "BOW, wow, wow! BOW, WOW!"

The Farmer heard the loud barks and jumped out of bed. Taking his gun, he leapt to the window and shouted: "What's the matter?"

"The thieves are here," answered Pinocchio.

"Where are they?"

"In the chicken coop."

"I'll come down in a second."

And, in fact, he was down in the yard in a twinkling and running toward the chicken coop.

He opened the door, pulled out the Weasels one by one, and, after tying them in a bag, said to them in a happy voice: "You're in my hands at last!"

Then he went up to Pinocchio and began to pet and caress him.

"Fine boy!" cried the Farmer, slapping him on the shoulder in a friendly way. "You ought to be proud of yourself. And to show you what I think of you, you are free from this instant!"

And he slipped the dog collar from his neck.

"Fine boy!" cried the Farmer.

PINOCCHIO WEEPS
UPON LEARNING THAT
THE *Lovely Maiden*
IS DEAD

⁕⁕⁕

HE MEETS A PIGEON,
WHO CARRIES HIM TO
THE SEASHORE

CHAPTER THIRTEEN

As soon as Pinocchio no longer felt the shameful weight of the dog collar around his neck, he started to run across the fields and meadows, and never stopped till he came to the main road that was to take him to the Fairy's house.

Running as fast as he could, he finally came to the spot where it had once stood. The little house was no longer there. In its place lay a small marble slab, which bore this sad inscription:

HERE LIES

THE LOVELY FAIRY WITH AZURE HAIR

WHO DIED OF GRIEF WHEN ABANDONED BY

Her Little Brother Pinocchio

A large pigeon flew far above Pinocchio.

The poor Marionette was heartbroken at reading these words. He fell to the ground and, covering the cold marble with kisses, burst into bitter tears. He cried all night, and dawn found him still there, though his tears had dried and only hard, dry sobs shook his wooden frame. But these were so loud that they could be heard by the faraway hills.

As he sobbed he said to himself:

"Oh, my Fairy, my dear, dear Fairy, why did you die? Why did I not die, who am so bad, instead of you, who are so good? And my father—where can he be? Please dear Fairy, tell me where he is and I shall never, never leave him again!"

Poor Pinocchio! He even tried to tear his hair, but as it was only painted on his wooden head, he could not even pull it.

Just then a large Pigeon flew far above him. Seeing the Marionette, he cried to him:

"Tell me," asked the Pigeon, "do you by chance know of a Marionette, Pinocchio by name?"

"Pinocchio! Did you say Pinocchio?" replied the Marionette, jumping to his feet. "Why, I am Pinocchio!"

At this answer, the Pigeon flew swiftly down to the earth. He was much larger than a turkey.

"Then you know Geppetto also?"

"Do I know him? He's my father, my poor, dear father! Has he, perhaps, spoken to you of me? Will you take me to him? Is he still alive? Answer me, please! Is he still alive?"

"I left him three days ago on the shore of a large sea."

"What was he doing?"

"He was building a little boat with which to cross the ocean. For the last four months, that poor man has been wandering around Europe, looking for you. Not having found you yet, he has made up his mind to look for you in the New World, far across the ocean."

"How far is it from here to the shore?" asked Pinocchio anxiously.

"More than fifty miles."

"Fifty miles? Oh, dear Pigeon, how I wish I had your wings!"

The next morning they were at the seashore.

The little boat was tossed about by the angry waters.

"If you want to come, I'll take you with me."

"How?"

"Astride my back. Are you very heavy?"

"Heavy? Not at all. I'm only a feather."

"Very well."

Saying nothing more, Pinocchio jumped on the Pigeon's back and, as he settled himself, he cried out gaily: "Gallop on, gallop on, my pretty steed! I'm in a great hurry."

The Pigeon flew away, and in a few minutes he had reached the clouds. The next morning they were at the seashore.

Pinocchio jumped off the Pigeon's back, and the Pigeon, not wanting any thanks for a kind deed, flew away swiftly and disappeared.

The shore was full of people, shrieking and tearing their hair as they looked toward the sea.

"What has happened?" asked Pinocchio of a little old woman.

"A poor old father lost his only son some time ago and today he built a tiny boat for himself in order to go in search of him across the ocean. The water is very rough and we're afraid he will be drowned."

"Where is the little boat?"

"There. Straight down there," answered the little old woman, pointing to a tiny shadow, no bigger than a nutshell, floating on the sea. Pinocchio looked closely for a few minutes and then gave a sharp cry:

"It's my father! It's my father!"

Meanwhile, the little boat, tossed about by the angry waters, appeared and disappeared in the waves. And Pinocchio, standing on a high rock, tired out with searching, waved to him with hand and cap and even with his nose.

It looked as if Geppetto, though far away from the shore, recognised his son, for he took off his cap and waved also. He seemed to be trying to make everyone understand that he would come back if he were able, but the sea was so heavy that he could do nothing with his oars. Suddenly a huge wave came and the boat disappeared.

They waited and waited for it, but it was gone.

Just then a desperate cry was heard. Turning around, the fisher folk saw Pinocchio dive into the sea and heard him cry out:

"I'll save him! I'll save my father!"

The Marionette, being made of wood, floated easily along and swam like a fish in the rough water. Spurred on by the hope of finding his father and of being in time to save him, he swam all night long.

At dawn, he saw, not far away from him, a long stretch of sand. It was an island in the middle of the sea.

PINOCCHIO

Reaches the Island
of the Busy Bees

AND FINDS THE FAIRY
ONCE MORE

CHAPTER FOURTEEN

PINOCCHIO TRIED HIS BEST to get there, but he couldn't. The waves played with him and tossed him about as if he were a twig or a bit of straw. At last, and luckily for him, a tremendous wave tossed him to the very spot where he wanted to be.

Little by little the sky cleared. The sun came out in full splendour and the sea became as calm as a lake.

Then the Marionette took off his clothes and laid them on the sand to dry. He looked over the waters to see whether he might catch sight of a boat with a little man in it.

The idea of finding himself in so lonesome a spot made him so sad that he was about to cry, but just then he saw a big Fish swimming nearby, with his head far out of the water.

Not knowing what to call him, the Marionette said to him:

"Hey there, Mr. Fish, may I have a word with you?"

"Even two, if you want," answered the fish, who happened to be a very polite Dolphin.

"Will you please tell me if, on this island, there are places where one may eat without necessarily being eaten?"

"Surely, there are," answered the Dolphin. "In fact you'll find one not far from this spot."

"And how shall I get there?"

"Take that path on your left and follow your nose. You can't go wrong."

"Tell me another thing. You who travel day and night through the sea, did you not perhaps meet a little boat with my father in it?"

"And who is you father?"

"He is the best father in the world, even as I am the worst son that can be found."

"In the storm of last night," answered the Dolphin, "the little boat must have been swamped."

"And my father?"

"By this time, he must have been swallowed by the Terrible Shark, which, for the last few days, has been bringing terror to these waters."

"Is this Shark very big?" asked Pinocchio, who was beginning to tremble with fright.

"Is he big?" replied the Dolphin. "Just to give you an idea

of his size, let me tell you that he is larger than a five-storey building and that he has a mouth so big and so deep, that a whole train and engine could easily get into it."

"Mother mine!" cried the Marionette, scared to death. This said, he took the path at so swift a gait that he seemed to fly, and at every small sound he heard, he turned in fear to see whether the Terrible Shark, five storeys high and with a train in his mouth, was following him.

After walking a half hour, he came to a small country called the Land of the Busy Bees. The streets were filled with people running to and fro about their tasks. Everyone worked, everyone had something to do. Even if one were to search with a lantern, not one idle man or one tramp could have been found.

"I understand," said Pinocchio at once wearily, "this is no place for me! I was not born for work."

But in the meantime, he began to feel hungry, for it was twenty-four hours since he had eaten.

What was to be done?

There were only two means left to him in order to get a bite to eat. He had either to work or to beg.

He was ashamed to beg, because his father had always preached to him that begging should be done only by the sick or the old. He had said that the real poor in this world, deserving of our pity and help, were only those who, either through age or sickness, had lost the means of earning their bread with their own hands. All others should work, and if they didn't, and went hungry, so much the worse for them.

Just then a man passed by, worn out and wet with perspiration, pulling, with difficulty, two heavy carts filled with coal. Pinocchio looked at him and, judging him by his looks to be a kind man, said to him with eyes downcast in shame:

"Will you be so good as to give me a penny, for I am faint with hunger?"

"Not only one penny," answered the Coal Man. "I'll give you four if you will help me pull these two wagons."

"Will you be so good as to give me a penny?"

"I am surprised!" answered the Marionette, very much offended. "I wish you to know that I never have been a donkey, nor have I ever pulled a wagon."

"So much the better for you!" answered the Coal Man. "Then, my boy, if you are really faint with hunger, eat two slices of your pride; and I hope they don't give you indigestion."

In less than a half hour, at least twenty people passed and Pinocchio begged of each one, but they all answered:

"Aren't you ashamed? Instead of being a beggar in the streets, why don't you look for work and earn your own bread?"

Finally a little woman went by carrying two water jugs.

"Good woman, will you allow me to have a drink from one of your jugs?" asked Pinocchio, who was burning up with thirst.

"With pleasure, my boy!" she answered, setting the two jugs on the ground before him.

When Pinocchio had had his fill, he grumbled, as he wiped his mouth: "My thirst is gone. If I could only as easily get rid of my hunger!"

On hearing these words, the good little woman immediately said: "If you help me to carry these jugs home, I'll give you a slice of bread. And with the bread, I'll give you a nice dish of cauliflower with white sauce on it. And after the cauliflower, some cake and jam."

Pinocchio could no longer resist and said firmly:

"Very well. I'll take the jug home for you."

The jug was very heavy, and the Marionette, not being strong enough to carry it with his hands, had to put it on his head.

When they arrived home, the little woman made Pinocchio sit down at a small table and placed before him the bread, the cauliflower, and the cake. Pinocchio did not eat; he devoured. His stomach seemed a bottomless pit.

His hunger finally appeased, he raised his head to thank his kind benefactress. But he had not looked at her long when he gave a cry of surprise and sat there with his eyes wide open, his fork in the air, and his mouth filled with bread and cauliflower.

"Why all this surprise?" asked the good woman, laughing.

"Because–" answered Pinocchio, stammering and stuttering, "because–you look like–you remind me of–yes, yes, the same voice, the same eyes, the same hair–yes, yes, yes, you also have the same azure hair she had–Oh, my little Fairy, my little Fairy! Tell me that it is you! Don't make me cry any longer! If you only knew! I have cried so much, I have suffered so!"

And Pinocchio threw himself on the floor and clasped the knees of the mysterious little woman.

"Oh, my little Fairy! Tell me that is you."

PINOCCHIO

promises to be good and to study, as he is growing tired of being a Marionette, and wishes to become...

A REAL BOY

CHAPTER FIFTEEN

"YOU RASCAL OF A MARIONETTE! How did you know it was I?" she asked, laughing.

"My love for you told me who you were."

"Do you remember? You left me when I was a little girl and now you find me a grown woman. I am so old, I could almost be your mother!"

"I am very glad of that, for then I can call you mother instead of sister. For a long time I have wanted a mother, just like other boys. But how did you grow so quickly? Look at me! I have never grown higher than a penny's worth of cheese."

"But you can't grow," answered the Fairy. "Marionettes never grow. They are born Marionettes, they live Marionettes, and they die Marionettes."

"Oh, I'm tired of always being a Marionette!" cried Pinocchio disgustedly. "It's about time for me to grow into a man as everyone else does."

"And you will if you deserve it—"

"Really? What can I do to deserve it?"

"It's a very simple matter. Try to act like a well-behaved child."

"Don't you think I do?"

"Good boys love study and work, but you—"

"And I, on the contrary, am a lazy fellow and a tramp all year round."

"Good boys always tell the truth."

"And I always tell lies."

"Good boys go gladly to school."

"And I get sick if I go to school. From now on I'll be different."

"Do you promise?"

"I promise. I want to become a good boy and be a comfort to my father. Will I ever be lucky enough to find him and embrace him once more?"

"I think so. Indeed, I am sure of it."

At this answer, Pinocchio's happiness was very great. He grasped the Fairy's hands and kissed them so hard that it looked as if he had lost his head.

"Beginning tomorrow," said the Fairy, "you'll go to school every day." Pinocchio's face fell a little. "Then you will choose the trade you like best." Pinocchio became more serious.

"It seems too late for me to go to school now."

"No, indeed. Remember it is never too late to learn."

"But I don't want either trade or profession."

"Why?"

"Because work wearies me!"

"My dear boy," said the Fairy, "people who speak as you do usually end their days either in a prison or in a hospital."

"I'll work; I'll study; I'll do all you tell me. After all, the life of a Marionette has grown very tiresome to me and I want to become a boy, no matter how hard it is. You promise that, do you not?"

"Yes, I promise, and now it is up to you."

In the morning, bright and early, Pinocchio started for school.

Imagine what the boys said when they saw a Marionette enter the classroom! They laughed until they cried. Everyone played tricks on him. One pulled his hat off, another tugged at his coat, a third tried to paint a mustache under his nose. One even attempted to tie strings to his feet and his hands to make him dance.

But, as the days passed into weeks, even the teacher praised him, for he saw him attentive, hard-working, and wide-awake, always the first to come in the morning, and the last to leave when school was over.

Pinocchio's only fault was that he had too many friends.

As the days passed into weeks, the teacher praised Pinocchio.

Among these were many well-known rascals, who cared not a jot for study or for success. The teacher warned him each day, and even the good Fairy repeated to him many times:

"Take care, Pinocchio! Those bad companions will sooner or later make you lose your love for study. Some day they will lead you astray."

"There's no such danger," answered the Marionette, shrugging his shoulders and pointing to his forehead as if to say, "I'm too wise."

So it happened that one day, as he was walking to school, he met some boys who ran up to him and said:

"Have you heard the news?"

"No!"

"A Shark as big as a mountain has been seen near the shore."

"Really? I wonder if it could be the same one I heard of when my father was drowned?"

"We are going to see it. Are you coming?"

"No, not I. I must go to school."

"What do you care about school? You can go there tomorrow. With a lesson more or less, we are always the same donkeys."

"Do you know what I'll do?" said Pinocchio. "For certain reasons of mine, I, too, want to see that Shark; but I'll go after school. I can see him then as well as now."

"Poor simpleton!" cried one of the boys. "Do you think that a fish of that size will stand there waiting for you? He turns and off he goes, and no one will ever be the wiser."

"How long does it take from here to the shore?" asked the Marionette.

"One hour there and back."

"Very well, then. Let's see who gets there first!" cried Pinocchio.

Pinocchio led the way, running as if on wings, the others following as fast as they could.

Going like the wind, Pinocchio took but a very short time to reach the shore. He glanced all about him, but there was no sign of a Shark.

THE GREAT BATTLE

Between Pinocchio and his playmates

ONE IS WOUNDED; PINOCCHIO IS ARRESTED.

CHAPTER SIXTEEN

THE SEA was as smooth as glass.

"Hey there, boys! Where's that Shark?" he asked, turning to his playmates.

"He may have gone for his breakfast," said one of them, laughing.

"Or, perhaps, he went to bed for a little nap," said another, laughing also.

From the answers and the laughter which followed them, Pinocchio understood that the boys had played a trick on him.

"What now?" he said angrily to them. "What's the joke?"

"Oh, the joke's on you!" cried his tormentors, laughing more heartily than ever, and dancing gayly around the Marionette.

"Don't you see? If you study and we don't, we pay for it. After all, it's only fair to look out for ourselves."

"Really, you amuse me," answered the Marionette, nodding his head.

"Hey, Pinocchio," cried the tallest of them all, "that will do. We are tired of hearing you bragging about yourself, you little turkey-cock! You may not be afraid of us, but remember we are not afraid of you, either! You are alone, you know, and we are seven. You'll go home with a broken nose!"

"Cuck–oo!"

"Very well, then! Take that, and keep it for your supper," called out the boldest of his tormentors. And with the words, he gave Pinocchio a terrible blow on the head.

Pinocchio answered with another blow, and that was the signal for the beginning of the fray. Readers, geographies, histories, grammars flew in all directions. But Pinocchio was keen of eye and swift of movement, and the books only passed over his head, landed in the sea, and disappeared.

The fish, thinking they might be good to eat, came to the top of the water in great numbers. Some took a nibble, some took a bite, but no sooner had they tasted a page or two, than they spat them out with a wry face, as if to say: "What a horrid taste! Our own food is so much better!"

In the meantime, the boys, having used all their books, looked around for new ammunition. Seeing Pinocchio's bundle lying idle nearby, they somehow managed to get hold of it.

The book struck one of the boys.

One of the books was a very large volume, an arithmetic text, heavily bound in leather. It was Pinocchio's pride. Among all his books, he liked that one the best.

Thinking it would make a fine missile, one of the boys took hold of it and threw it with all his strength at Pinocchio's head. But instead of hitting the Marionette, the book struck one of the other boys, who, as pale as a ghost, cried out faintly: "Oh, Mother, help! I'm dying!" and fell senseless to the ground.

Scared to death by the horror of what had been done, Pinocchio ran to the sea and soaked his handkerchief in the cool water and with it bathed the head of his poor little school-mate. Sobbing bitterly, he called to him, saying:

"Eugene! My poor Eugene! Open your eyes and look at me! Why don't you answer? I was not the one who hit you, you know. Believe me, I didn't do it. Open your eyes, Eugene!"

Pinocchio went on crying and moaning and beating his head. Again and again he called to his little friend, when suddenly he heard heavy steps approaching.

He looked up and saw two tall Carabineers near him.

"What are you doing stretched out on the ground?" they asked Pinocchio.

"I'm helping this school-fellow of mine."

"This boy has been wounded on the temple" said one of the Carabineers. "Who has hurt him? And with what was he wounded?"

"With this book," and the Marionette picked up the arithmetic text to show it to the officer.

"And whose book is this?"

"Mine."

"Enough. Not another word! Get up as quickly as you can and come along with us."

They then took hold of Pinocchio and, putting him between them, said to him in a rough voice: "March! And go quickly, or it will be the worse for you!"

They had just reached the village, when a sudden gust of wind blew off Pinocchio's cap and made it go sailing far down the street.

"Would you allow me," the Marionette asked the Carabineers, "to run after my cap?"

"Very well, go; but hurry."

The Marionette went, picked up his cap—but instead of putting it on his head, he stuck it between his teeth and then raced toward the sea. He went like a bullet out of a gun.

The Carabineers, judging that it would be very difficult to catch him, sent Alidoro, a large Mastiff after him, one that had won first prize in all the dog races. Pinocchio ran fast and the Dog ran faster.

Luckily, by this time, he was very near the shore, and the sea was in sight; in fact, only a few short steps away.

As soon as he set foot on the beach, Pinocchio gave a leap and fell into the water. Alidoro tried to stop, but as he was running very fast, he couldn't, and he, too, landed far out in the sea.

"Help, Pinocchio, dear little Pinocchio! Save me from death!"

At those cries of suffering, the Marionette, who after all had a very kind heart, was moved to compassion. He turned toward the poor animal and said to him: "But if I help you, will you promise not to bother me again by running after me?"

"I promise! I promise! Only hurry, for if you wait another second, I'll be dead and gone!"

Pinocchio hesitated still another minute. Then, remembering

Pinocchio dragged Alidoro to the shore.

how his father had often told him that a kind deed is never lost, he swam to Alidoro and, catching hold of his tail, dragged him to the shore.

The poor Dog was so weak he could not stand. He had swallowed so much salt water that he was swollen like a balloon. However, Pinocchio, not wishing to trust him too much, threw himself once again into the sea. As he swam away, he called out: "Goodbye, Alidoro, good luck and remember me to the family!"

"Goodbye, little Pinocchio," answered the Dog. "A thousand thanks for having saved me from death. You did me a good turn, and, in this world, what is given is always returned. If the chance comes, I shall be there."

Pinocchio went on swimming close to shore. At last he thought he had reached a safe place. Glancing up and down the beach, he saw the opening of a cave out of which rose a spiral of smoke.

"In that cave," he said to himself, "there must be a fire. So much the better. I'll dry my clothes and warm myself, and then—well—"

His mind made up, Pinocchio swam to the rocks, but as he started to climb, he felt something under him lifting him up higher and higher. He tried to escape, but he was too late. To his great surprise, he found himself in a huge net, amid a crowd of fish of all kinds and sizes, who were fighting and struggling

Pinocchio found himself in a huge net, amid a crowd of fish.

desperately to free themselves.

At the same time, he saw a Fisherman come out of the cave. When the Fisherman pulled the net out of the sea, he cried out joyfully:

"Blessed Providence! Once more I'll have a fine meal of fish!"

"Thank Heaven, I'm not a fish!" said Pinocchio to himself, trying with these words to find a little courage.

The Fisherman took the net and the fish to the cave, a dark, gloomy, smoky place. In the middle of it, a pan full of oil sizzled over a smoky fire, sending out a repelling odour of tallow that took away one's breath.

"Now, let's see what kind of fish we have caught today," said the Fisherman. He put a hand as big as a spade into the net and pulled out a handful of mullets and whitefish and flounders and crabs and...

The last to come out of the net was Pinocchio.

As soon as the Fisherman pulled him out, he cried out in fear: "What kind of fish is this? I don't remember ever eating anything like it."

"Beware how you deal with me!" said Pinocchio. "I am a Marionette, I want you to know."

"A Marionette?" asked the Fisherman. "I must admit that a Marionette fish is, for me, an entirely new kind of fish. So much the better. I'll eat you with greater relish."

"Eat me? But can't you understand that I'm not a fish? Can't you hear that I speak and think as you do?"

"Well, as a sign of my particular esteem for you, I'll leave to you the choice of the manner in which you are to be cooked. Do you wish to be fried in a pan, or do you prefer to be cooked with tomato sauce?"

"To tell you the truth," answered Pinocchio, "if I must choose, I should much rather go free so I may return home!"

"Are you fooling? Do you think that I want to lose the opportunity to taste such a rare fish?"

The unlucky Marionette, hearing this, began to cry and wail and beg.

And as he struggled and squirmed like an eel to escape from him, the Fisherman took a stout cord and tied him hand and foot, and threw him into the bottom of the tub with the others.

Then he pulled a wooden bowl full of flour out of a cupboard and started to roll the fish into it, one by one.

He started to roll the fish into the bowl of flour, one by one.

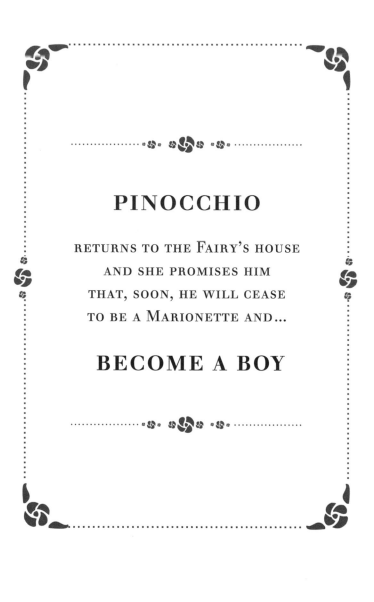

PINOCCHIO

RETURNS TO THE FAIRY'S HOUSE
AND SHE PROMISES HIM
THAT, SOON, HE WILL CEASE
TO BE A MARIONETTE AND...

BECOME A BOY

CHAPTER SEVENTEEN

MINDFUL OF what the Fisherman had said, Pinocchio knew that all hope of being saved had gone. He closed his eyes and waited for the final moment.

Suddenly, a large Dog, attracted by the odour of the boiling oil, came running into the cave.

"Get out!" cried the Fisherman threateningly and still holding onto the Marionette, who was all covered with flour.

And he drew back his foot to give the Dog a kick. Then the Dog, who, being really hungry, would take no refusal, turned in a rage toward the Fisherman and bared his terrible fangs. And at that moment, a pitiful little voice was heard saying: "Save me, Alidoro; if you don't, I fry!"

The Dog immediately recognised Pinocchio's voice. Then what did he do? With one great leap, he grasped that bundle in

The dog grasped Pinocchio in his mouth.

"How much do I thank you!" said the Marionette.

his mouth and, holding it lightly between his teeth, ran through the door and disappeared like a flash!

"How much I do thank you!" said the Marionette.

"It is not necessary," answered the Dog. "You saved me once, and what is given is always returned. We are in this world to help one another."

"But how did you get in that cave?"

"I was lying here on the sand more dead than alive, when an appetising odour of fried fish came to me."

"Don't speak about it," wailed Pinocchio, still trembling with fright. "Don't say a word. If you had come a moment later, I would be fried, eaten, and digested by this time. Brrrrr! I shiver at the mere thought of it."

Alidoro and he then bid each other goodbye and the Dog went home.

Pinocchio, left alone, decided to go back to the Blue Fairy. He came to the village late at night. It was so dark he could see nothing and it was raining pitchforks.

Pinocchio went straight to the Fairy's house, firmly resolved to knock at the door.

When he found himself there, he lost courage and ran back a few steps. A second time he came to the door and again he ran back. A third time he repeated his performance. He gave up finally and decided to wait for her to appear.

He waited and waited and waited. Finally, after a full half hour, a top-floor window (the house had four storeys) opened and Pinocchio saw a large Snail look out. A tiny light glowed on top of her head. "Who knocks at this late hour?" she called.

"Is the Fairy home?" asked the Marionette.

"The Fairy is asleep and does not wish to be disturbed. Who are you?"

"Pinocchio. The Marionette; the one who lives in the Fairy's house."

"Oh, I understand," said the Snail. "Wait for me there. I'll come down to open the door for you."

"Hurry, I beg of you, for I am dying of cold."

"My boy, I am a snail and snails are never in a hurry."

An hour passed, two hours; and the door was still closed. Then Pinocchio, losing all patience, stepped back and gave the door a most solemn kick. He kicked so hard that his foot went straight through the door and his leg followed almost to the knee. No matter how he pulled and tugged, he could not pull it out. There he stayed as if nailed to the door.

Poor Pinocchio! The rest of the night he had to spend with one foot through the door and the other one in the air.

As dawn was breaking, the door finally opened. That brave little animal, the Snail, had taken exactly nine hours to go from the fourth floor to the street.

"What are you doing with your foot through the door?" she asked the Marionette, laughing.

"It was a misfortune. Won't you try, pretty little Snail, to free me from this terrible torture?"

"My boy, we need a carpenter here and I have never been one."

"Ask the Fairy to help me!"

"The Fairy is asleep and does not want to be disturbed."

Pinocchio wanted to cry, he wanted to give himself up to despair. Instead, either from pain or weakness, he fell to the floor in a dead faint.

When he regained his senses, he found himself stretched out

"My boy, snails are never in a hurry."

on a sofa and the Fairy was seated near him.

"This time also I forgive you," said the Fairy to him. "But be careful not to get into mischief again."

Pinocchio promised to study and to behave himself. And he kept his word for the remainder of the year. At the end of it, he passed first in all his examinations, and his report was so good that the Fairy said to him happily: "Tomorrow your wish will come true."

"And what is it?"

"Tomorrow you will cease to be a Marionette and will become a real boy."

Pinocchio was beside himself with joy. All his friends and

schoolmates must be invited to celebrate the great event! The Fairy promised to prepare two hundred cups of coffee-and-milk and four hundred slices of toast buttered on both sides. Pinocchio asked for permission to give out the invitations.

"Indeed, you may invite your friends to tomorrow's party. Only remember to return home before dark. Do you understand?"

"I'll be back in one hour without fail," answered the Marionette.

Without adding another word, the Marionette bade the good Fairy goodbye, and singing and dancing, he left the house.

In a little more than an hour, all his friends were invited. Now it must be known that, among all his friends, Pinocchio had one whom he loved most of all. The boy's real name was Romeo, but everyone called him Lamp-Wick, for he was long and thin and had a woebegone look about him.

PINOCCHIO

instead of becoming
a boy, runs away to

THE LAND OF TOYS

with his friend,
Lamp-Wick

CHAPTER EIGHTEEN

LAMP-WICK WAS THE LAZIEST BOY in the school and the biggest mischief-maker, but Pinocchio loved him dearly. That day, he went straight to his friend's house to invite him to the party, but Lamp-Wick was not at home. Where could he be? Pinocchio searched here and there and everywhere, and finally discovered him hiding near a farmer's wagon.

"What are you doing there?" asked Pinocchio, running up to him.

"I am waiting for midnight to strike to go—"

"Where?"

"To a real country—the best in the world—a wonderful place!"

"What is it called?"

"It is called the Land of Toys. Why don't you come, too?"

"I? Oh, no!"

Lamp-Wick was the laziest boy in the school.

"You are making a big mistake, Pinocchio. Believe me, if you don't come, you'll be sorry. No schools, no teachers, no books! In that blessed place there is no such thing as study. In the Land of Toys, every day, except Sunday, is a Saturday. Vacation begins on the first of January and ends on the last day of December. That is the place for me!"

"But how does one spend the day in the Land of Toys?"

"Days are spent in play and enjoyment from morning till night. At night one goes to bed, and next morning, the good times begin all over again. What do you think of it?"

"No, no, and again no! I have promised my kind Fairy to become a good boy, and I want to keep my word."

"Wait two minutes more."

"Are you going alone or with others?"

"Alone? There will be more than a hundred of us! At midnight the wagon passes here that is to take us within the boundaries of that marvellous country."

"Listen, Lamp-Wick," said the Marionette, "are you really sure that there are no schools in the Land of Toys?"

"Not even the shadow of one."

"Not even one teacher?"

"Not one."

"What a great land!" said Pinocchio, feeling his mouth water. "What a beautiful land! I have never been there, but I can well imagine it."

With these words, the Marionette started on his way home. Turning once more to his friend, he asked him: "But are you sure that, in that country, each week is composed of six Saturdays and one Sunday?"

In the meantime, the night became darker and darker. All at once in the distance a small light flickered. A queer sound could be heard, soft as a little bell, and faint and muffled like the buzz of a far away mosquito.

"There it is!" cried Lamp-Wick, jumping to his feet. "The wagon which is coming to get me!"

Finally the wagon arrived. It made no noise, for its wheels were bound with straw and rags. It was drawn by twelve pairs of donkeys, all of the same size, but all of different colour. Some were grey, others white, and still others a mixture of brown and black. Here and there were a few with large yellow and blue stripes.

The strangest thing of all was that those twenty-four donkeys, instead of being iron-shod like any other beast of burden, had on their feet laced shoes made of leather, just like the ones boys wear.

And the driver of the wagon? Imagine to yourselves a little, fat man, much wider than he was long, round and shiny as a ball of butter, with a face beaming like an apple, a little mouth that always smiled, and a voice small and wheedling like that of a cat begging for food.

No sooner had the wagon stopped than the little fat man turned to Lamp-Wick. With bows and smiles, he asked in a wheedling tone: "Tell me, *my fine boy*, do you also want to come to my *wonderful* country?"

"Indeed I do."

"But I warn you, *my little dear,* there's no more room in the wagon. It is full."

"Never mind," answered Lamp-Wick. "If there's no room inside, I can sit on the top of the coach."

And with one leap, he perched himself there.

"What about *you, my love?*" asked the Little Man, turning politely to Pinocchio. "What are you going to do? *Will you come with us,* or do you stay here?"

"I stay here," answered Pinocchio. "I want to return home, as I prefer to study and to succeed in life."

"Come with us and we'll always be happy," cried four other voices from the wagon.

"Come with us and we'll always be happy," shouted the one hundred and more boys in the wagon, all together.

Pinocchio did not answer, but sighed deeply once—twice—a third time. Finally, he said:

"Make room for me. I want to go, too!"

Pinocchio mounted and the wagon started its way.

Pinocchio mounted and the wagon started on its way. While the donkeys galloped along the stony road, the Marionette fancied he heard a very quiet voice whispering to him: " POOR SILLY ! YOU HAVE DONE AS YOU WISHED. BUT YOU ARE GOING TO BE A SORRY BOY BEFORE VERY LONG. "

Pinocchio, greatly frightened, looked about him to see whence the words had come, but he saw no-one.

Soon, they were in the Land of Toys. Its population, large though it was, was composed wholly of boys. The oldest were about fourteen years of age, the youngest, eight. In the street, there was such a racket, such shouting, such blowing of trumpets, that it was deafening.

As soon as they had set foot in that land, Pinocchio, Lamp-Wick, and all the other boys who had travelled with them started out on a tour of investigation. They wandered everywhere, they looked into every nook and corner, house and theatre. They became everybody's friend. Who could be happier than they? What with entertainments and parties, the hours, the days, the weeks passed like lightning.

Five months passed and the boys continued playing and enjoying themselves from morn till night, without ever seeing a book, or a desk, or a school.

The boys continued enjoying themselves from morning till night.

After Five Months of Play

**PINOCCHIO'S EARS BECOME
LIKE THOSE OF A DONKEY.**

In a Little While

**HE BECOMES A DONKEY
AND STARTS TO BRAY**

CHAPTER NINETEEN

THERE CAME A MORNING when Pinocchio awoke and found a great surprise awaiting him! He found that, during the night, his ears had grown at least ten full inches! He went in search of a mirror, but not finding any, he just filled a basin with water and looked at himself. There he saw what he never could have wished to see. His manly figure was adorned and enriched by a beautiful pair of donkey's ears.

I leave you to think of the terrible grief, the shame, the despair of the poor Marionette.

He began to cry, to scream, to knock his head against the wall, but the more he shrieked, the longer and the more hairy grew his ears. At those piercing shrieks, a Dormouse came into the room. He took Pinocchio's wrist between her paws and, after a few minutes, looked up at him sorrowfully and said: "My

Pinocchio's figure was adorned by a pair of donkey's ears.

friend, I am sorry, but I must give you some very sad news."

"What is it?"

"You have a very bad fever."

"But what fever is it?"

"The donkey fever. Within two or three hours, you will no longer be a Marionette, nor a boy. You'll turn into a donkey. Just like the ones that pull the fruit carts to market."

"Oh, what have I done? What have I done?" cried Pinocchio, grasping his two long ears in his hands and pulling and tugging at them angrily, just as if they belonged to another.

"My dear boy," answered the Dormouse to cheer him up a bit, "Why worry now? What is done cannot be undone, you know. Fate has decreed that all lazy boys who come to hate books and schools and teachers and spend all their days with toys and games must sooner or later turn into donkeys."

"But is it really so?" asked the Marionette, sobbing bitterly.

"I am sorry to say it is. And tears now are useless. You should have thought of all this before."

"But the fault is not mine. Believe me, little Dormouse, the fault is all Lamp-Wick's."

"Well, now, look out for Lamp-wick!" warned the Dormouse and went his way.

Pinocchio walked to the door of the room and looked about for his friend. But not before he covered his ears with a paper cover. Imagine his surprise when he saw him, with a large cotton bag on his head, pulled far down to his very nose.

The two lads looked at each other long and hard.

"Well" said the Marionette breaking the silence. "Let us take off our caps together. Shall we?"

"All right."

Pinocchio began to count, "One! Two! Three!"

At the word "Three!" the two boys pulled off their caps and threw them high in air.

And then a scene took place which is hard to believe, but it is all too true. The Marionette and his friend, Lamp-Wick, when they saw each other both stricken by the same misfortune, instead of feeling sorrowful and ashamed, began to poke fun at each other, and after much nonsense, they ended by bursting out into hearty laughter.

But all of a sudden Lamp-Wick stopped laughing. He tottered and almost fell. Pinocchio too felt his legs give way. Soon, both of them fell on all fours and began running and jumping around the room. This was humiliation enough, but the most horrible moment was the one in which the two poor creatures felt their tails appear. Overcome with shame and grief, they tried to cry and bemoan their fate.

At that moment, a loud knocking was heard at the door of their house and a voice called to them:

After months of play and no work, they became donkeys.

"Open! I am the Little Man, the driver of the wagon which brought you here. Open, I say, or beware!"

The Little Man did not wait for them to come to the door. He gave it such a violent kick that it flew open. He smiled at the two and said: "Fine work, boys! You have brayed well, so well that I recognised your voices immediately, and here I am."

And now do you understand what the Little Man's profession was? This horrid little being, whose face shone with kindness, went about the world looking for boys. Lazy boys, boys who hated books, boys who wanted to run away from home, boys who were tired of school—all these were his joy and his fortune. He took them with him to the Land of Toys and let them enjoy themselves to their heart's content. When, after months of all play and no work, they became little donkeys, he sold them on the market place. In a few years, he had become a millionaire.

Poor Pinocchio was sold to a circus-master. After putting him in a stable, his new master filled his manger with straw, but Pinocchio, after tasting a mouthful, spat it out.

Then the man filled the manger with hay. But Pinocchio did not like that any better.

"Ah, you don't like hay either?" he cried angrily. "Wait, my pretty Donkey, I'll teach you not to be so particular."

Without more ado, he took a whip and gave the Donkey a hearty blow across the legs.

Pinocchio screamed with pain and as he screamed he brayed: "Haw! Haw! Haw! I can't digest straw!"

"Then eat the hay!" answered his master, who understood the Donkey perfectly.

"Haw! Haw! Haw! Hay gives me a headache!"

"Do you pretend, by any chance, that I should feed you duck or chicken?" asked the man again, and, angrier than ever, he gave poor Pinocchio another lashing and left him to his own devices.

Finally, not finding anything else in the manger, he tasted the hay. After tasting it, he chewed it well, closed his eyes, and swallowed it.

"This hay is not bad," he said to himself. "But how much happier I should be if I had studied! Just now, instead of hay, I should be eating some good bread and butter. Patience!"

Poor Pinocchio, whether he liked it or not, had to get through other difficulties. He had to learn to waltz, dance the polka, stand on his head...

The day came at last when Pinocchio's master was able to announce an extraordinary performance. The announcements, posted all around the town, and written in large letters, read thus:

+ GREAT SPECTACLE TONIGHT +
LEAPS AND EXERCISES BY THE GREAT ARTIST
AND THE FAMOUS HORSES OF THE COMPANY
FIRST PUBLIC APPEARANCE OF THE FAMOUS DONKEY CALLED
Pinocchio
+ THE STAR OF THE DANCE +
THE THEATRE WILL BE AS LIGHT AS DAY

That night, as you can well imagine, the theatre was filled to overflowing one hour before the show was scheduled to start. Soon, the circus-master led Pinocchio to the stage.

"Most honoured audience! I shall not take your time tonight to tell you of the great difficulties which I have encountered while trying to tame this animal, since I found him in the wilds of Africa. Observe, I beg of you, the savage look of his eye. All the means used by centuries of civilization in subduing wild beasts failed in this case. I had finally to resort to the gentle language of the whip in order to bring him to my will. Admire him, O gentlemen, and enjoy yourselves."

The Master bowed and then turned to Pinocchio and said: "Ready, Pinocchio! Start!"

A shower of applause greeted the Donkey as he finished his show. At all that noise, Pinocchio lifted his head and raised his eyes. There, in front of him, in a box sat a beautiful woman. Around her neck she wore a long gold chain, from which hung a large medallion. On the medallion was painted the picture of a Marionette.

"That picture is of me! That beautiful lady is my Fairy!" said Pinocchio to himself, recognising her. He felt so happy that he tried his best to cry out: "Oh, my Fairy! My own Fairy!"

But instead of words, a loud braying was heard in the theatre, so loud and so long that all the spectators—men, women, and children, but especially the children—burst out laughing.

Then, in order to teach the Donkey that it was not good manners to bray before the public, the Master hit him on the nose with the handle of the whip.

The poor little Donkey stuck out a long tongue and licked

his nose for a long time in an effort to take away the pain. And what was his grief when on looking up toward the boxes, he saw that the Fairy had disappeared! He felt himself fainting, his eyes filled with tears, and he wept bitterly. He could not do anything more that evening, and when his master tried to put him through the ring, he broke his leg! "What do I want with a lame donkey?" said the Circus Master to his stableboy. "Take him to the market and sell him."

When they reached the square, a buyer agreed to pay four pennies for the donkey. But that was not the end of the Donkey's misfortunes. His new owner took him to a high cliff overlooking the sea, put a stone around his neck, tied a rope to one of his hind feet, gave him a push, and threw him into the water.

Pinocchio sank immediately. And his new master sat on the cliff waiting for him to drown, so as to skin him and make himself a drumhead.

PINOCCHIO

IS THROWN INTO THE SEA,
EATEN BY FISHES, AND
BECOMES A MARIONETTE
ONCE MORE

AS HE SWIMS TO LAND,
HE IS SWALLOWED BY

THE TERRIBLE
SHARK

CHAPTER TWENTY

Down into the sea, deeper and deeper, sank Pinocchio, and finally, after fifty minutes of waiting, the man on the cliff said to himself:

"By this time my poor little lame Donkey must be drowned. Up with him and then I can get to work on my beautiful drum."

He pulled the rope which he had tied to Pinocchio's leg–pulled and pulled and pulled and, at last, he saw appear on the surface of the water–Can you guess what? Instead of a dead donkey, he saw a very much alive Marionette, wriggling and squirming like an eel.

Seeing that wooden Marionette, the poor man thought he was dreaming and sat there with his mouth wide open and his eyes popping out of his head. Gathering his wits together, he said:

"And the Donkey I threw into the sea?"

"I am that Donkey," answered the Marionette laughing.

'But, then, how is it that you, who a few minutes ago were a donkey, are now standing before me a wooden Marionette?"

"It may be the effect of salt water. The sea is fond of playing these tricks."

"Be careful, Marionette, be careful! Don't laugh at me! Woe be to you, if I lose my patience!"

"Well, then, my Master, do you want to know my whole story? Untie my leg and I can tell it to you better."

The old fellow, curious to know the true story of the Marionette's life, immediately untied the rope which held his foot. Pinocchio, feeling free as a bird of the air, told him his tale. Just as he finished his story, Pinocchio decided that he would not wait to find out the old man's reactions. He gave a quick leap and dived into the sea. Swimming away as fast as he could, he cried out, laughing:

"Goodbye, Master. If you ever need a skin for your drum, remember me."

In a few seconds he had gone so far he could hardly be seen. After swimming for a long time, Pinocchio saw a large rock in the middle of the sea, a rock as white as marble. High on the rock stood a little Goat bleating and calling and beckoning to the Marionette to come to her.

There was something very strange about that little Goat. Her coat was not white or black or brown as that of any other goat, but azure, a deep brilliant colour that reminded one of the hair of the lovely maiden. Pinocchio's heart beat fast, and then faster and faster. He redoubled his efforts and swam as hard as he could toward the white rock. He was almost halfway over, when suddenly a horrible sea monster stuck its head out of the water, an enormous head with a huge mouth, wide open, showing three rows of gleaming teeth, the mere sight of which would have filled you with fear. Do you know what it was?

That sea monster was no other than the enormous Shark, which has often been mentioned in this story and which, on account of its cruelty, had been nicknamed *The Attila of the Sea* by both fish and fishermen. Poor Pinocchio! The sight of that monster frightened him almost to death! He tried to swim away from him, to change his path, to escape, but that immense mouth kept coming nearer and nearer.

"Hasten, Pinocchio, I beg you!" bleated the little Goat on the high rock.

And Pinocchio swam desperately with his arms, his body, his legs, his feet.

But the monster overtook him and the Marionette found himself in between the rows of gleaming white teeth. The Monster swallowed him so fast that Pinocchio, falling down into the body of the fish, lay stunned for a half hour.

The Monster swallowed him so fast.

"But I don't want to be digested," said Pinocchio.

When he recovered his senses the Marionette could not remember where he was. Around him all was darkness, a darkness so deep and so black that for a moment he thought he had put his head into an inkwell.

Pinocchio at first tried to be brave, but as soon as he became convinced that he was really and truly in the Shark's stomach, he burst into sobs and tears. "Help! Help!" he cried. "Oh, poor me! Won't someone come to save me?"

"Who is there to help you, unhappy boy?" said a rough voice, like a guitar out of tune.

"Who is talking?" asked Pinocchio, frozen with terror.

"It is I, a poor Tunny swallowed by the Shark at the same time as you.

And what kind of a fish are *you?*"

"I have nothing to do with fishes. I am a Marionette."

"If you are not a fish, why did you let this monster swallow you?"

"I didn't let him. He chased me and swallowed me without even a 'by your leave!' And now what are we to do here in the dark?"

"Wait until the Shark has digested us both, I suppose."

"But I don't want to be digested," shouted Pinocchio, starting to sob.

"Neither do I," said the Tunny, "but I am wise enough to think that if one is born a fish, it is more dignified to die under the water than in the frying pan."

"Is this Shark that has swallowed us very long?" asked the Marionette.

"His body, not counting the tail, is almost a mile long."

While talking in the darkness, Pinocchio thought he saw a faint light in the distance.

"What can that be?" he said to the Tunny.

"Some other poor fish, waiting as patiently as we to be digested by the Shark."

"I want to see him. He may be an old fish and may know some way of escape."

"I wish you all good luck, dear Marionette."

"Goodbye, Tunny."

"Goodbye, Marionette, and good luck."

Pinocchio tottered away in the darkness and began to walk as well as he could toward the faint light which glowed in the distance.

The farther on he went, the brighter and clearer grew the tiny light. On and on he walked till finally he found–I give you a thousand guesses, my dear children! He found a little table set for dinner and lighted by a candle stuck in a glass bottle; and near the table sat a little old man, white as the snow, eating live fish. They wriggled so that, now and again, one of them slipped out of the old man's mouth and escaped into the darkness under the table.

At this sight, the poor Marionette was filled with such great and sudden happiness that he almost dropped in a faint. He wanted to laugh, he wanted to cry, he wanted to say a thousand and one things, but all he could do was to stand still, stuttering and stammering brokenly. At last, with a great effort, he was able to let out a scream of joy and, opening wide his arms he threw them around the old man's neck.

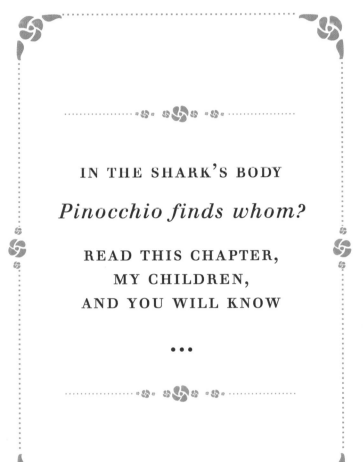

IN THE SHARK'S BODY

Pinocchio finds whom?

READ THIS CHAPTER,
MY CHILDREN,
AND YOU WILL KNOW

...

CHAPTER TWENTY-ONE

"OH, FATHER, DEAR FATHER! Have I found you at last? Now I shall never, never leave you again!"

"Are my eyes really telling me the truth?" answered the old man, rubbing his eyes. "Are you really my own dear Pinocchio?"

"Yes, yes, yes! It is I! Look at me! And you have forgiven me, haven't you? Oh, my dear Father, how good you are! And to think that I—Oh, but if you only knew how many misfortunes have fallen on my head…"

And Pinocchio proceeded to narrate all that had befallen him. He ended with him trying to save his father from drowning.

"I remember that," put in Geppetto, "and I wanted to go to you; but how could I? The sea was rough and the whitecaps overturned the boat. Then a Terrible Shark came up out of the sea and, as soon as he saw me in the water, swam quickly toward me, put out his tongue, and swallowed me as easily as if I had been a chocolate peppermint."

"And how long have you been shut away in here?"

"From that day to this, two long weary years—two years, my Pinocchio, which have been like two centuries."

"And how have you lived? Where did you find the candle? And the matches with which to light it—where did you get them?"

"Oh Father, dear Father! Have I found you at last?"

"You must know that, in the storm which swamped my boat, a large ship also suffered the same fate. The sailors were all saved, but the ship went right to the bottom of the sea, and the same Terrible Shark that swallowed me, swallowed most of it."

"What! Swallowed a ship?" asked Pinocchio in astonishment.

"To my own good luck, that ship was loaded with meat, preserved foods, crackers, bread, bottles of wine, raisins, cheese, coffee, sugar, wax candles, and boxes of matches. With all these blessings, I have been able to live happily on for two whole years, but now I am at the very last crumbs…"

"Then, my dear Father," said Pinocchio, "there is no time to lose. We must try to escape. We can run out of the Shark's mouth and dive into the sea."

"You speak well, but I cannot swim, my dear Pinocchio."

"Why should that matter? You can climb on my shoulders and I, who am a fine swimmer, will carry you safely to the shore."

"Dreams, my boy!" answered Geppetto, shaking his head and smiling sadly. "Do you think it possible for a Marionette, a yard high, to have the strength to carry me on his shoulders and swim?"

"Try it and see! And in any case, if it is written that we must die, we shall at least die together."

Not adding another word, Pinocchio took the candle in his hand and going ahead to light the way, he said to his father: "Follow me and have no fear."

They walked a long distance through the stomach and the whole body of the Shark. When they reached the throat of the monster, they stopped for a while to wait for the right moment in which to make their escape.

I want you to know that the Shark, being very old and suffering from asthma and heart trouble, was obliged to sleep with his mouth open. Because of this, Pinocchio was able to catch a glimpse of the sky filled with stars, as he looked up through the open jaws of his new home.

"The time has come for us to escape," he whispered, turning to his father. "The Shark is fast asleep. The sea is calm and the night is as bright as day. Follow me closely, dear Father, and we shall soon be saved."

No sooner said than done. They climbed up the throat of the monster till they came to that immense open mouth. There they had to walk on tiptoes, for if they tickled the Shark's long tongue he might awaken—and where would they be then? The tongue was so wide and so long that it looked like a country road. They crossed it however and jumped over three rows of teeth. But before they took the last great leap, the Marionette said to his father: "Climb on my back and hold on tightly to my neck. I'll take care of everything else."

As soon as Geppetto was comfortably seated on his shoulders, Pinocchio, very sure of what he was doing, dived into the water and started to swim. The sea was like oil, the moon shone in all splendour, and the Shark continued to sleep so soundly that not even a cannon shot would have awakened him.

Pinocchio dived into the water and started to swim.

PINOCCHIO

*finally ceases to
be a Marionette
and becomes*

A Boy !

CHAPTER TWENTY-TWO

"My dear Father, we are saved!" cried the Marionette. "All we have to do now is to get to the shore, and that is easy."

Without another word, he swam swiftly away in an effort to reach land as soon as possible.

"I see the shore," said the Marionette. "Remember, Father, that I am like a cat. I see better at night than by day."

Poor Pinocchio pretended to be peaceful and contented, but he was far from that. He was beginning to feel discouraged, his strength was leaving him, and his breathing was becoming more and more laboured.

Father and son were really about to drown when they heard a voice like a guitar out of tune call from the sea:

"What is the trouble?"

"It is I and my poor father. I can't swim anymore and we

"I am the Tunny, your companion in the Shark's stomach."

are drowning!"

"Oh, it's you, Pinocchio."

"Exactly. And you?"

"I am the Tunny, your companion in the Shark's stomach."

"And how did you escape?"

"I imitated your example. You are the one who showed me the way and after you went, I followed. Look, hang onto my tail, both of you, and let me lead you. In a twinkling you will be safe on land."

Geppetto and Pinocchio, as you can easily imagine, did not refuse the invitation; indeed, instead of hanging onto the tail, they thought it better to climb on the Tunny's back.

"Are we too heavy?" asked Pinocchio.

Pinocchio thought it best to climb onto the Tunny's back.

"Heavy? Not in the least. You are as light as sea-shells," answered the Tunny, who was as large as a two-year-old horse.

As soon as they reached the shore, Pinocchio was the first to jump to the ground to help his old father. Then he turned to the fish and said to him:

"Dear friend, you have saved my father, and I have not enough words with which to thank you! Allow me to embrace you as a sign of my eternal gratitude."

The Tunny stuck his nose out of the water and Pinocchio knelt on the sand and kissed him most affectionately on his cheek.

In the meantime day had dawned.

Pinocchio offered his arm to Geppetto, who was so weak he could hardly stand, and said to him:

"Lean on my arm, dear Father, and let us go. We will walk very, very slowly, and if we feel tired we can rest by the wayside."

They had not taken a hundred steps when they saw two rough-looking individuals sitting on a stone begging for alms.

It was the Fox and the Cat, but one could hardly recognise them, they looked so miserable. The Cat, after pretending to be blind for so many years had really lost the sight of both eyes. And the Fox, old, thin, and almost hairless, had even lost his tail. That sly thief had fallen into deepest poverty, and one day he had been forced to sell his beautiful tail for a bite to eat.

"Oh, Pinocchio," he cried in a tearful voice. "Give us some

alms, we beg of you! We are old, tired, and sick."

"Sick!" repeated the Cat.

"Goodbye, false friends!" answered the Marionette. "You cheated me once, but you will never catch me again."

Waving goodbye to them, Pinocchio and Geppetto calmly went on their way. After a few more steps, they saw, at the end of a long road near a clump of trees, a tiny cottage built of straw.

They went and knocked at the door.

"Who is it?" said a little voice from within.

"A poor father and a poorer son, without food and with no roof to cover them," answered the Marionette.

"Turn the key and the door will open," said the same little voice.

Pinocchio turned the key and the door opened. As soon as they went in, they looked here and there and everywhere but saw no one.

"Oh–ho, where is the owner of the hut?" cried Pinocchio, very much surprised.

"Here I am, up here!"

Father and son looked up to the ceiling, and there on a beam sat the Talking Cricket.

"Oh, my dear Cricket," said Pinocchio, bowing politely.

"Oh, now you call me your dear Cricket, but do you remember when you threw your hammer at me to kill me?"

"You are right, little Cricket, you are more than right, and I

"Oh, my dear Cricket," said Pinocchio, bowing politely.

shall remember the lesson you have taught me. But will you tell how you succeeded in buying this pretty little cottage?"

"This cottage was given to me yesterday by a little Goat with blue hair."

"And where did the Goat go?" asked Pinocchio.

"I don't know."

"And when will she come back?"

"She will never come back. Yesterday she went away bleating sadly, and it seemed to me she said: "Poor Pinocchio, I shall never see him again... the Shark must have eaten him by this time."

"Were those her real words? Then it was she—it was—my dear

175

little Fairy," cried out Pinocchio, sobbing bitterly.

"Tell me, little Cricket, where shall I find a glass of milk for my poor Father?"

"Three fields away from here lives Farmer John. He has some cows. Go there and he will give you what you want."

Pinocchio ran all the way to Farmer John's house. The Farmer said to him:

"How much milk do you want?"

"I want a full glass."

"You have to earn that glass. Go to that well you see yonder and draw one hundred bucketfuls of water. After you have finished, I shall give you a glass of warm sweet milk."

"I am satisfied."

Farmer John took the Marionette to the well and showed him how to draw the water. Pinocchio set to work as well as he knew how, but long before he had pulled up the one hundred buckets, he was tired out and dripping with perspiration. Farmer John gave him his glass of milk and Pinocchio went back to his father.

From that day on, for more than five months, Pinocchio got up every morning just as dawn was breaking and went to the farm to draw water. And every day he was given a glass of warm milk for his poor old father, who grew stronger and better day by day. But he was not satisfied with this. He learnt to make

Pinocchio learned to make baskets of reed and sold them.

baskets of reeds and sold them. With the money he received, he and his father were able to keep from starving.

Among other things, he built a rolling chair, strong and comfortable, to take his old father out for an airing on bright, sunny days.

In the evening the Marionette studied by lamplight. With some of the money he had earned, he bought himself a secondhand volume that had a few pages missing, and with that he learnt to read in a very short time. As far as writing was concerned, he used a long stick at one end of which he had whittled a long, fine point. Ink he had none, so he used the juice of blackberries or cherries   Little by little his diligence was rewarded. He succeeded, not only in his studies, but also in his work, and a day came when he put enough money together to keep his old father comfortable and happy. Besides this, he was able to save the great amount of fifty pennies. With it he wanted to buy himself a new suit.

One day he said to his father: "I am going to the market place to buy myself a coat, a cap, and a pair of shoes. When I come back I'll be so dressed up, you will think I am a rich man."

He ran out of the house and up the road to the village, laughing and singing. Suddenly he heard his name called, and looking around to see whence the voice came, he noticed a large snail crawling out of some bushes.

"Don't you recognize me?" said the Snail.

"Yes and no."

"Do you remember the Snail that lived with the Fairy with Azure Hair? Do you not remember how she opened the door for you one night and gave you something to eat?"

"I remember everything," cried Pinocchio. "Answer me quickly, pretty Snail, where have you left my Fairy? What is she doing? Has she forgiven me? Does she remember me? Does she still love me? Is she very far away from here? May I see her?"

At all these questions, tumbling out one after another, the Snail answered, calm as ever:

"My dear Pinocchio, the Fairy is lying ill in a hospital."

"In a hospital?"

"Yes, indeed. She has been stricken with trouble and illness, and she hasn't a penny left with which to buy a bite of bread."

"Really? Oh, how sorry I am! My poor, dear little Fairy! If I had a million I should run to her with it! But I have only fifty pennies. Here they are. I was just going to buy some clothes. Here, take them, little Snail, and give them to my good Fairy."

The Snail, much against her usual habit, began to run like a lizard under a summer sun.

When Pinocchio returned home, his father asked him: "And where is the new suit?"

"I couldn't find one to fit me. I shall have to look again some other day."

That night, Pinocchio, instead of going to bed at ten o'clock waited until midnight, and instead of making eight baskets, he made sixteen.

After that he went to bed and fell asleep. As he slept, he dreamt of his Fairy, beautiful, smiling, and happy, who kissed him and said to him, "Bravo, Pinocchio! In reward for your kind heart, I forgive you for all your old mischief. Boys who love and take good care of their parents when they are old and sick, deserve praise even though they may not be held up as models of obedience and good behaviour. Keep on doing so well, and you will be happy."

That night, Pinocchio made sixteen baskets.

At that very moment, Pinocchio awoke and opened wide his eyes. What was his surprise and his joy when, on looking himself over, he saw that he was no longer a Marionette, but that he had become a real live boy! He looked all about him and instead of the usual walls of straw, he found himself in a beautifully furnished little room, the prettiest he had ever seen.

In a twinkling, he jumped down from his bed to look on the chair standing near. There, he found a new suit, a new hat, and a pair of shoes. As soon as he was dressed, he put his hands in his pockets and pulled out a little leather purse on which were written the following words:

The Fairy with Azure Hair RETURNS FIFTY PENNIES TO HER DEAR PINOCCHIO WITH MANY THANKS FOR HIS KIND HEART.

"And where is Father?" he cried suddenly. He ran into the next room, and there stood Geppetto, grown years younger overnight, spick and span in his new clothes and gay as a lark in the morning. He was once more Mastro Geppetto, the wood carver, hard at work on a lovely picture frame, decorating it with flowers and leaves, and heads of animals.

"Father, Father, what has happened? Tell me if you can," cried Pinocchio, as he ran and jumped on his Father's neck.

"This sudden change in our house is all your doing, my dear Pinocchio," answered Geppetto.

As he slept, he dreamt of his Fairy.

"What have I to do with it?"

"Just this. When bad boys become good and kind, they have the power of making their homes gay and new with happiness."

"I wonder where the old Pinocchio of wood has hidden himself?"

"There he is," answered Geppetto. And he pointed to a large Marionette leaning against a chair, head turned to one side, arms hanging limp, and legs twisted under him. After a long, long look, Pinocchio said to himself with great content, "How ridiculous I was as a Marionette! And how happy I am now that I have become a real boy!"

THE END

RE-DRAWING A CLASSIC

The idea for *The Patua Pinocchio* emerged out of a workshop conceived by Tara Books, with artists from the Patua tradition of painting in Bengal. This is a folk form which combines painting, story-telling and performance: the story is recited or sung as the performer holds up a painted scroll, pointing to the image that goes with his or her words. We have an ongoing interest in connecting Indian picture story-telling traditions with narratives from across the world, and one of our most exciting dialogues has been with Patua artists.

Patua artists are keenly interested in stories of all kinds, from contemporary news to fables and legends from diverse contexts. Their pictorial imagination re-casts received tales into their own familiar aesthetic idiom, and as a result, older symbols and motifs are constantly updated, acquiring ever newer meanings.

One of the artists who took part in our workshop was Swarna Chitrakar, a well-known woman artist who has been painting scrolls for over twenty years. From the many stories that were circulated in the workshop, Swarna chose to work with the tale of Pinocchio, the naughty Italian marionette whose adventures have delighted generations of children and adults

Swarna Chitrakar, Self-portrait

across the world. His mischievous character reminded her of the popular Hindu god Krishna, whose childhood exploits have been the subject of literature, art and song. So she renders Pinocchio as a lovable yet godly trickster figure from Hindu lore—a naughty but essentially beatific child who looks composed and serene at all times.

Typically, in Patua art, the story unfolds through a series of panels, with images sometimes flowing across several panels. For this project, Swarna worked with the single panel as a unit, and so every piece of action or character remains within one frame. Some images combine theme, character and movement in a single composition—those that depict Pinocchio's adventures in the sea are examples of this.

While adapting the conventions of Patua art to the form of the book, Swarna has retained some typical tropes of her tradition, especially with respect to clothing. Pinocchio is sometimes half-clad, and at other times he sports only jewellery. His friends too are half-clad much of the time, wearing only the cloth that Pinocchio also wears now and then.

In Patua art, clothing and accessories are not meant to be realistic–so within a single sequence, a character might wear differently coloured clothes. In this tradition, as in many others in India, clothes perform a different function–they identify a social type. The fisherman's turban is an example of clothing that marks a well-defined social group. Clothing also marks social status. Poor people such as Geppetto, the coal-man and the fisherman, like Pinocchio, are humbly clad. Powerful men such as the master carpenter, Antonio, the director of the Marionette Theatre, the schoolmaster, the cruel carriage driver and the Carabineers are fully and almost regally clad. The Blue Fairy wears the Indian sari, as many rural women do, but her blue hair and occasional jewellery grants her a special status. In the event, she is both homely as well as goddess-like–not unlike baby Krishna's mother. Interestingly, Swarna has chosen to depict her as strong and nurturing, rather than as delicate and gentle.

Patua artists specialize in figures of birds and animals, and Swarna was particularly taken with the character of the sly Cat. In the folk traditions that she has grown up with, the cat stands in for a self-satisfied and unctuous being, and in *The Patua Pinocchio* the Cat is at once comic and menacing. Her birds are likewise drawn from an existing repertoire. Patua art also features a variety of fish, and Swarna has given us a particularly resplendent shark. Where the tradition does not yield her prototypes, she has imagined them for herself with great power and clarity, as in her depiction of the Talking Cricket.

The Patua Pinnochio emerged out of a workshop process, and took shape through an ongoing dialogue between the artist and the Tara editorial and design team. The text was adapted from the original English translation of Collodi's Italian text, and edited in ways that would allow the illustrations their place. While working with Swarna's illustrations, designer Tanuja Ramani decided to foreground the bold outlines and iconic features characteristic of Patua art. She also decided to retain the borders that marked each of Swarna's panels, to complement the text. The patterned endpapers are likewise based on these border motifs. In keeping with the 'classical' status of the text, the layout is reminiscent of late 19th century design, with type and printers' ornaments used to reference a classic storybook aesthetic, along with subtle typeplay.

This is the first time that Patua art has been used to illustrate a children's classic from another tradition. While re-drawing and designing the tale, the book adds fresh–and startlingly unfamiliar–layers of meaning to a well-known story, and in the process, renders it truly universal.

V. Geetha
Tara Books

The Patua Pinocchio
Copyright © 2014 Tara Books Private Limited

For the original text: Carlo Collodi
Edited by: V. Geetha
For the illustrations: Swarna Chitrakar

For this edition: Tara Publishing Ltd., UK | www.tarabooks.com/uk
Tara Books Pvt. Ltd., India | www.tarabooks.com

Design: Tanuja Ramani
Production: C. Arumugam
Printed in China by Leo Paper and Products.

ISBN: 978-93-83145-12-6

The Patua Pinocchio is an edited and abridged version of Carol Della Chiesa's
translation from the Italian.